Stranded on a far-flung planet in the dark space between galaxies, the Earthmen had little hope for survival. The ship and its communications system were wrecked, and now that the twilight planet's inhabitants had discovered the Earthmen's blasphemous presence—they were as good as doomed.

For the dread Ai Chun would not believe the Earthmen's story: that they came by starship from *another* world countless light-years away.

This was not possible, the ancient Ai Chun insisted, for their planet was the *only* world: the world created by themselves, the omnipotent god race of the universe. How could the Earthmen hope to challenge a race of gods . . . ? Moreover, a race of gods who could and would enslave them . . . and destroy their minds in the process.

POUL ANDERSON was born in Bristol, Pennsylvania, and was graduated as a physics major from the University of Minnesota. Writing was a hobby of his, and he sold a few stories while in college. With jobs hard to find after graduation, he continued to write and found to his surprise that he was not a scientist at all, but a born writer. Best known for his science-fiction, he has also written mysteries, non-fiction and historical novels.

Poul Anderson lives in Orinda, California, with his wife and daughter. Novels of his published in Ace Books editions include:

MAYDAY ORBIT   (F-104)

THE MAKESHIFT ROCKET   (F-139)

LET THE SPACEMEN BEWARE!   (F-209)

STAR WAYS   (D-568)

WAR OF THE WING-MEN   (D-303)

WORLD
WITHOUT
STARS

by

POUL ANDERSON

ACE BOOKS, INC.
1120 Avenue of the Americas
New York, N.Y. 10036

I

GOD WAS RISING in the west, and this time the sun was down—only lately, a few clouds were still red above the eastern treetops, against purple dusk; but over the hours that light had waned, until it was little more than an echo of what now swung above Lake Silence—so that His pale glory stood clear to be adored.

The Pack could not all make worship. They had met on a ridge near the lairs and howled when the fingers of God's foremost arm glimmered into view. But He would take long to mount so high that His entire self was revealed. The hes must hunt, the shes wreak, the youngs gather, lest God's Coursers perish. Moreover and worse, the whole Pack unmoving here, so distant from their hills, could draw the notice of a downdevil out of the sea depths; and night or no, the downdevil might then send a war fleet of the Herd . . . if, indeed, that which had lately arrived in fire and thunder was not enemy work itself. Ya-Kela, the One, had brought some bold followers who would go with him to see about that. But first he stood his watch of homage on behalf of the whole folk.

5

Slowly, slowly, God climbed into heaven. Ya-Kela crouched on the back of Crooked Rock and sang. He sang the Welcome, and the Praise, and the Strength. Then the last coals of sunset went out, and the sky was empty of everything save God, the angels, and three planets, and God cast a white glade from the world's edge, down the width of Lake Silence until it was lost among the reeds at this shore. The night was still and cool. A breeze gusted, smelling of damp; a fish leaped in a single clear splash, a wing cried its lonely note, reeds rustled and were answered by the inland brush; but otherwise ya-Kela and God had darkness to themselves.

He stopped a while to rest and eat. He was hoarse, the rock was harsh beneath his webs and tail, and weariness dragged at him. *Yes,* he thought, *I grow old. But I am yet the One of the Pack.* —A distant boom made him start. Drums? It was not impossible for the Herd to come raiding by night. But it was rare. The downdevils feared God and so their worshipers did too. . . . *Only a twyhorn, off in Umber Swamp,* he decided.

He looked west again, and was astonished to see God's body flame in sight. *Why, I must have dozed,* he thought in dismay. *Does that mean anything other than that I am in truth old?* Hastily he went through the invocations and gestures he had missed, until he was caught up. The legends haunted him about creatures that had long ago come from the sky and returned—to Herd day or Pack night, who knew save God and the downdevils? Were these unknown newcomers at Balefire Head, whom he must presently seek out, the same ones? More than ever, the world needed shielding against strangeness. "I call to Thee, we call to Thee, Thou Who casteth out the sun, arise, arise, arise . . . . "

II

ON ANOTHER EVENING, very far away, I had heard another song. This was when I got back to City.

Like most who colonize a planet, the settlers of Landomar wanted nature and elbow room. There is no other good reason for planting yourself at the bottom of a gravity well. The reason is not quite logical—after all, most of us can satisfy our ape instincts with an occasional groundside visit somewhere, or just with a multisense tape—but I suppose that a gene complex still crops up occasionally which makes the owner want to belong to a specific patch of earth. So if you can find a habitable uninhabited world (statistically rare, but consider how many stars the universe holds) you go with a band of like-minded people to claim it. I don't know whether breeding then reinforces the instinct, or the original parents remain culturally dominant over the centuries. In all events, after a while you have a scattered population which doesn't want outsiders building a starport.

At the same time, starports are necessary. Theoretically they shouldn't be, when any point in space is as close as any other point. In practice, though, an expanding race needs them. First, you have to make up energy differentials between one system and the next in stages. That's obvious enough in the case of the really remote galaxies; we could get there, but we couldn't match a relative velocity which is a goodly fraction of c. However, just the variation between, say, the inner and outer part of a spiral arm is a bit too fuel-consuming to overcome in a single jump.

Then second, you need a base for observation, so you can

7

establish precisely where your next goal is and how fast it's moving. And third, of course, you want docks, yards, supply depots. Those could be built anywhere, but since the advanced bases are required for the first two reasons, they soon serve the third function also. And the fourth: rest, recreation, a place to roister and brag and ease off. For this purpose, even a spaceman born is happiest when the environment isn't entirely artificial.

They were more reasonable on Landomar than on some worlds I could name. They wouldn't let us build on the ground, but they made no objection to an orbital satellite. We could go down to their villages and farmsteads, hunt in their forests, sail on their oceans. They didn't mind our money in the least. Then, as City got bigger, with more and more to offer, their young folk started coming to us, to visit, eventually to work. The elders grumbled, until we brought in sociodynamicists to extrapolate the trend for them and prove that it would never really affect their own timeless oneness with the planet. At most, a cluster of small space-oriented service enterprises would develop groundside. Which is what happened.

I had spent several days there, arranging for stores, isotopes, and so forth. I also hoped to recruit a gunner. But in that I'd failed. Those few who applied ≈ d no aptitude. Well, there was a man, a hunter by trade; but the psychograph showed that he enjoyed killing too much. I felt a little tired and depressed. It didn't help, either, that Wenli was ill. Nothing serious, but the kid would doubtless be adult when I returned, and I like to remember my get as happy while they're small.

So I was eager to leave dust behind. My boat hit sky with a yell. Landomar became a giant cloud-banded shield, soft blue against the black. Before long City hove in view.

You can't add randomly to a satellite, or the spin properties would get ridiculous. But City had existed for a few centuries now, and grown in a way that the Landomar elders would not admit was organic. I remembered the original cheerless metal shell. Today I saw towers rocketing from parapets, domes and ports glowing brighter than stars, the Ramakan memorial rakish across the galactic clouds; I could see ships in dock and boats aswarm; and as nearly as any spaceman (except Hugh Valland) ever does, I felt I was home.

I cycled through the lockfield faster than was strictly safe and did no more than tell the mechmen to check out an irregularity which had registered in the boat-pilot's gamma rhythm. At once, wreck all formality, I was out of the dock area and its crowds, along the ramps and through the halls toward Lute's place.

She lives in high-weight, overlooking space itself. That's expensive, but her husbands can afford to pay their share. Not that she picks them on any such basis—not Lute—it's only that a handsome, intelligent woman attracts able men. She's probably my favorite portwife.

So I hurried down the last corridor. It was empty at the moment. My feet thudded on the floor, which gave me a springier response than Landomar's overrated lawns, and the ventilators seemed to purr louder than usual. The color patterns in the walls happened to be grays and greens, and that was right too; they fitted with the touch of sadness, homesickness-in-advance, which counterpointed my pleasure in getting back.

The music did likewise: so much so that I was almost on top of it before it registered on me. An omnisonor was being played, uncommonly well. The tune was archaic, paced like sea tides, but with ringing chords below; and then a man's voice joined in, quite softly:

"Mary O'Meara, the stars and the dewfall have covered your hilltop with light.

The wind in the lilies that blossom around you goes
bearin' your name from the height.
My girl, you are all of the night."

I rounded the hall's curve about the satellite and saw him.
He lounged in a bay close to Lute's door. The broad port
framed him in darkness and a crescent moon. His fingers ran
casually over the keys of the instrument in his lap, his eyes
were half closed and he was singing to himself.

"A ship out of shadow bears homeward by starlight, by
stars and the loom of your hill.
A hand at a brow is uplifted in peerin', salutin' and
shakin' with chill.
My dear, are you waitin' there still?"

In a pause for breath, he noticed me. Something I did not
understand went out of his face, to be replaced by a friendly
grin. "Hello," he said. His accent had an odd lilt. "Sorry
about the racket."

"Enjoyable, sir," I answered formally.

"I was passin' the time," he said, "waitin' for Captain
Argens."

"Myself." I bowed.

He unsprawled his height, which was considerable, and
thrust out a muscular hand. Archaic for certain! But I made
the clasp, and took that moment to study him.

His dress was conventional: blue tunic, white breeks, flexi-
ble halfboots. The comets of a Master's rating glowed on his
wide shoulders. But the physical type was one that you don't
see often: fair skin over craggy features, close-cropped yellow
hair, fire-blue eyes. "Hugh Valland," he said, "off the *Lady
Lara.*"

"Felipe Argens," I responded, mechanically in my startle-

10

ment. I'm old enough to recognize that anyone bearing a name like his must be a great deal older.

"Hear you're lookin' for a gunner," he said.

"Well . . . yes." That was no surprise. Gossip flies fast when more than one ship is in port. "You're interested?"

"Yes, sir, I am. The *Lady's* inbound again, so her skipper don't mind lettin' me off my contract. Understand you're goin' to Earth."

"Eventually," I nodded. "Might be some time, though."

"That's all right. Just so we get there."

I made a fast computation. If this man had served on the *Lady* he'd have a record and shipmates to consult: much better than a psychograph. Though he already looked good.

"Fine; let's talk," I said. "But, uh, why didn't you wait in the apartment? My wife would have been glad—"

"Hear tell she's got a sick kid. Didn't know if she'd want to play hostess." I liked him better and better.

The door dilated for me and Lute met us. "How's Wenli?" I asked after presentations.

"Fretful," she said. "Fever. I had her down to the clinic and they confirmed it's a neovirus."

Nothing to be alarmed about, oh, no, not with supportive treatment. But when a thing that was extraterrestrial to start with mutates, the biotechs in a frontier post like City don't have the equipment to tailor a quick-cure molecule. In twenty years or so, having reached optimum adulthood, Wenli would get her antithanatic; thereafter her cells would instantly reject any hostile nucleic acids. But for now my little girl must rely on what poor defenses nature had provided. Recovery would be slow.

She was asleep. I peeked in at the flushed round face, then went back to the others. Valland was jollying Lute with an anecdote from his latest voyage. They'd needed to gain prestige in a culture which rated poetics as the highest art, so he'd introduced the limerick. Watching her laugh, I felt a

11

twinge of jealousy. Not personal; Lute is so thoroughly decent that it isn't even awkward when two of her men happen to be in port at the same time. No, I only wished I had Valland's gift of blarney.

Yet when we invited him to dinner, he accepted with a courtliness you rarely see anymore.

He and I went onto the porch for cocktails while Lute programmed the food mechs. Space dropped dizzily from the viewport, thin starred black here on the rim. Huge and shapeless—we being still more or less within it—the galaxy streamed past and was lost to sight; we looked toward remoteness.

"I need a gunner in case of trouble," I told him. "We'll be dealing with a technologically advanced race, one that we know almost nothing about. But of course we don't really expect a fight, so we want a man who can double as second deck officer. If he has some xenological skill to boot, that's ideal."

"I think I can claim the whole lot," he answered. "No formal trainin'. By the time they got around to foundin' academies in those subjects, I'd already been in space for quite a spell. But you can check me out with the people aboard *Lady Lara*, and on a psychograph too if you want."

Luck seemed to have fluxed in my direction. Unless—"You may change your mind when you know where the *Meteor's* bound," I warned him. "Or do you?"

"No. Just that it's a pretty long hop, and you'll call at Earth afterward. Otherwise none of your gang has blabbed." He chuckled. "Reckon you'd rather not have competition in the early stages of contact, when the cream's at its most skimmable."

"I'll have to tell you, though, and trust you as a Guild brother. We're going to some Yonderfolk."

"Eh?" He started gratifyingly. "Beyond this galaxy? Like M 31?"

"No," I said. "Not that far. Though where we're bound, we'll be much lonelier. Intergalactic space."

Valland settled back, crossed his legs and twirled his glass between calloused fingers. I offered him a cigarillo, but he declined in favor of a pipe from his tunic: another archaism. Having lit up, I explained:

"There are stars between the galaxies, you know. Dim red dwarfs, so widely separated that this neighborhood looks crowded by comparison; nevertheless, stars. Hitherto no one's thought it worthwhile to investigate them in any detail. Not when we'll take millions of years learning about this one Milky Way of our own, let alone its sisters. But lately . . . some of the intergalactics have made contact with us. They might be worth trading with, goods or knowledge or both. We're going out to have a look. If anything develops, we'll stay for a few years to get the business established."

"I see." He blew a slow cloud. "Sounds interestin'. But after that, you'll head for Earth?"

"Yes. A universarium there is one of the *Meteor's* co-owners, and wants a direct report." I shrugged. "Science is still alive on Earth, if nothing else."

"More'n that," he murmured. "Earth'll always be Manhome."

"Look here," I asked bluntly, "if you're so anxious to go back, why not get a ticket?"

"No hurry." His affability was unruffled. "I'd've done so in time, if need be. I've done it before. But passage across an energy gap like that isn't cheap. Might's well get paid for makin' the trip."

I didn't press him. That's no way to get to know a man. And I had to know my crew, so that we wouldn't break under the years of otherness.

Lute had arranged a good dinner. We were enjoying it, talking the usual things—whatever became of old Jarud, did you hear what happened on Claw, now once I met the damnedest nonhuman society you ever, let me warn you from bitter experience against gambling with the Stonks, is it true they've made a machine that—when Wenli came in. She was trying not to cry.

"Daddy!" she begged of me. "I got bad dreams in my head."

"Better start the hypnopulser, Lute," I muttered as I picked up the slight form. Having operated out of City enough consecutive years to know as well as beget the child, I hurt at her pain.

My wife half rose. " 'Scuse me, mistress," Valland said. "Don't you think best we chase the dreams off for good before we put her to sleep?"

She looked doubtful. "I been around a while," Valland said apologetically. "Not a father myself, but you can't help pilin' up observations. C'mere, little lady." He held out his arms and I passed Wenli to him.

He set her on his lap and leaned back from the table, letting the plate keep his food warm. "All right, my friend," he said, "what kind of dreams?"

She was at a shy stage of life, but to him she explained about blobby monsters that wanted to sit on her. "Well, now," he said, "I know a person who can take care of that. Let's ask him to come give a hand."

"Who?" Her eyes got quite round.

"Fellow name of Thor. He has a red beard, and he drives in a wagon pulled by goats—goats are animals with horns and long *long* whiskers—and the wheels make thunder. You ever heard thunder? Sounds like a boat takin' off in a terrible hurry. And Thor has a hammer, too, which he throws at trolls. I don't think those blobby characters will stand a chance."

I started to open my mouth. This didn't look semantically right to me. Lute laid a warning hand on mine. Following her gaze, I saw that Wenli had stopped shivering.

"Will Thor come if we ask?" she breathed.

"Oh, yes," Valland said. "He owes me a favor. I helped him out once when he got into an argument with an electrostatic generator. Now let me tell you more about him."

Afterward I learned that the tall tale he went on to relate came from Earth, in days so old that even the books are forgetting. But Wenli crowed and clapped her hands when Thor caught the snake that girdles the world. Lute laughed. So did I.

Finally Valland carried Wenli back to bed, fetched his omnisonor, and sang to her. The ballad was likewise ancient— his translation—but it bounced right along, and before he had finished cataloguing the improbable things that should be done to the drunken sailor, my daughter was asleep with no machine needed.

We came back to the 'fresher room. "Sorry to poke in like that," Valland said. "Maybe you should've curbed me."

"No." Lute's eyes glowed. "I've never seen anyone do anything better."

"Thanks. I'm a childish type myself, so—Hoy, meant to tell you before, this is one gorgeous piece of steak."

We went on to brandy and soda. Valland's capacity was epical. I suppose Lute and I were rather drunk toward the end, though we wouldn't have regretted it next day if our idea had been workable. We exchanged a glance, she nodded, and we offered our guest our total hospitality.

He hadn't shown much effect of alcohol, beyond merriment. Yet now he actually blushed. "No," he said. "Thanks a million, but I got me a berth in dock country. Better get down there."

Lute wasn't quite pleased. She has her human share of vanity. He saw that too. Rising, he took her hand and bowed above it.

"You see," he explained with great gentleness, "I'm from way back. The antithanatic was developed in my lifetime—

15

yes, that long ago; I shipped on the first star craft. So I have medieval habits. What other people do, fine, that's their business. But I've only got one girl, and she's on Earth."

"Oh," Lute said. "Haven't you been gone from her for quite a time, then?"

He smiled. "Sure have. Why do you think I want to return?"

"I don't understand why you left in the first place."

Valland took no offense. "Earth's no place for a live man to live any more. Fine for Mary, not for me. It's not unfair to either of us. We get together often enough, considerin' that we'll never grow old. Between whiles, I can remember . . . . But goodnight now, and thanks again."

His attitude still seemed peculiar to me. I'd have to check most carefully with his present captain. You can't take an unbalanced man out between the galaxies.

On the other hand, we're each a bit eccentric, one way or another. That goes along with being immortal. Sometimes we're a bit crazy, even. We don't have the heart to edit certain things out of our memories, and so they grow in the psyche till we no longer have a sense of proportion about them. Like my own case—but no matter.

One thing we have all gained in our centuries is patience. Could be that Hugh Valland simply had a bit more than most.

III

We were nine aboard the *Meteor*, specialists whose skills overlapped. That was not many, to rattle around in so huge a hull. But you need room and privacy on a long trip, and of course as a rule we hauled a lot of cargo.

"Probably not this time, however," I explained to Valland and Yo Rorn. They were the only ones who hadn't shipped with me before; I'd hastily recruited them at Landomar when two vacancies developed for reasons that aren't relevant here. To make up the delay, I hadn't briefed them in detail before we started. But now I must. They'd need days of study to master what little we knew about our goal.

We sat in my com chamber, we three, with coffee and smokes. A steady one gee of acceleration gave weight, and that soft engine-pulse which goes on and on until finally it enters your bones. A viewscreen showed us Landomar's sun, already dwindled, and the galaxy filling half the sky with clots and sprawls of glow. That was to starboard; the vector we wanted to build up ran almost parallel to the rim. Portward yawned emptiness, here and there the dim spindles of other stellar continents.

"Mmm, yeah, don't look like we could find a lot of useful stuff on a planet where they breathe hydrogen and drink liquid ammonia," Valland nodded. "I never did, anyway."

"Then why are we going?" Rorn asked. He was a lean, dark, saturnine man who kept to himself, hadn't so much as told us where in the cosmos he was born. His psychograph indicated a tightly checked instability. But the readings also

17

said he was a good electronician, and he had recommendations from past service. He stubbed out his cigaret and lit another. "Someone from a similar planet would be logical to deal with the—what did you say their name was?"

"I can't pronounce it either," I replied. "Let's just call them Yonderfolk."

Rorn scowled. "That could mean any extragalactic race."

"We know what we mean," said Valland mildly. "Ever meet the natives of Carstor's Planet?"

"Heard of them," I said. "Tall, thin, very ancient culture, unbearably dignified. Right?"

"Uh-huh. When I was there, we called 'em Squidgies."

"Business, please," Rorn barked.

"Very well," I said. "What we hope to get from our Yonderfolk is, mainly, knowledge. Insights, ideas, art forms, possibly something new in physics or chemistry or some other science. You never can tell. If nothing else, they know about the intergalactic stars, so maybe they can steer us onto planets that will be profitable for humans. In fact, judging from what they've revealed so far, there's one such planet right in their home system."

Valland looked for a while into the blackness to port. "They must be different from anybody we've met before," he murmured. "We can't imagine how different."

"Right," I said. "Consider what that could mean in terms of what they know."

I cleared my throat. "Brace yourself, Yo," said Valland. "The Old Man's shiftin' into lecture gear." Rorn looked blank, then resentful. I didn't mind.

"The galaxies were formed by the condensation of monstrous hydrogen clouds. But there wasn't an absolute vacuum between them. Especially not in the beginning, when the universe hadn't yet expanded very far. So between the proto-galaxies there must have been smaller condensations of gas, which became star clusters. Giant stars in those clusters soon went supernova, enriching the interstellar medium. Some second and third generation suns got born.

"But then the clusters broke up. Gravitational effect of the galaxies, you see. The dispersal of matter became too great for star formation to go on. The bright ones burned themselves out. But the red dwarfs are still around. A type M, for instance, stays fifty billion years on the main sequence."

"Please," Rorn said, irritated. "Valland and I do know elementary astrophysics." To the gunner: "Don't you?"

"But I begin to see what it means," Valland said low. Excitement coursed over his face. He clenched his pipe in one fist. "Stars so far apart that you can't find one from another without a big telescope. Metal poor, because the supernova enrichment stopped early. And old—old."

"Right," I said. "Planets, too. Almost without iron or copper or uranium, anything that made it so easy for us to become industrialized. But the lighter elements exist. So does life. So does intelligence.

"I don't know how those Yonderfolk we're going to visit went beyond the Stone Age. That's one of the things we have to find out. I can guess. They could experiment with electrostatics, with voltaic piles, with ceramics. Finally they could get to the point of electrodynamics—oh, let's say by using ceramic tubes filled with electrolytic solution for conductors. And so, finally, they'd extract light metals like aluminum and magnesium from ores. But they may have needed millions of years of civilization to get that far, and beyond."

"What'd they learn along the way?" Valland wondered. "Yeah, I see why we've got to go there."

"Even after they developed the space jump, they steered clear of the galaxies," I said. "They can't take the radiation. Where they live, there are no natural radioactives worth mentioning, except perhaps a few things like K-40. Their sun doesn't spit out many charged particles. There's no galactic magnetic field to accelerate cosmic rays. No supernovae either."

"Why, maybe they have natural immortality," Valland suggested.

"Mmm, I doubt that," I said. "True, we're saddled with more radiation. But ordinary quantum processes will mutate cells too. Or viruses, or chemicals, or Q factor, or—or whatever else they may have on Yonder."

"Have they developed an antithanatic, then?" Rorn asked.

"I don't know," I said. "If not, that's one valuable thing we have to offer. I hope."

I saw in the brief twist of Valland's mouth that he understood me. Spacemen don't talk about it much, but there are races, as intelligent and as able to suffer as we ourselves, for whom nobody has figured out an aging preventive. The job is hard enough in most cases: develop a synthetic virus which, rather than attacking normal cells, destroys any that do *not* quite conform to the host's genetic code. When the biochemistry is too different from what we know— Mostly, we leave such planets alone.

I said in haste: "But let's keep to facts. The Yonderfolk did at last venture to the galactic rim, with heavy radiation screening. It so happened that the first world they came on which was in contact with our civilization was Zara. Our own company had a factor there."

We didn't yet know how many suns they visited first. Our one galaxy holds more than a hundred billion, most of which have attendants. I doubt if we'll ever see them all. There could be any number of civilizations as great as ours, that close to home, unbeknownst to us. And yet we go hopping off to Andromeda!

(I made that remark to Hugh Valland, later in the voyage. "Sure," he said. "Always happens that way. The Spanish were settlin' the Philippines before they knew the coastal outline of America. People were on the moon before they'd got to

20

the bottom of the Mindanao Deep." At the time I didn't quite follow him, but since then I've read a little about the history of Manhome.)

"Zara." Rorn frowned. "I don't quite place—"

"Why should you?" Valland replied. "More planets around than you could shake a stick at. Though I really can't see why anybody'd want to shake a stick at a planet that never did him any harm."

"It's the same type as the Yonderfolk's home," I said. "Zara, that is. Cold, hydrogen-helium atmosphere, et cetera. They made contact with our factor because he was sitting in the only obviously machine-culture complex on the surface. They went through the usual linguistic problems, and finally got to conversing. Here's a picture."

I activated my projector and rotated the image of a being. It was no more inhuman than many who had been my friends: squat, scaly, head like a complicated sponge; one of several hands carried something which sparkled.

"Actually," I said, "the language barrier was higher than ordinary. To be expected, no doubt, when they came from such an alien environment. So we don't have a lot of information, and a good deal of what we do have must be garbled. Still, we're reasonably sure they aren't foolish enough to be hostile, and do want to develop this new relationship. Within the galaxy, they're badly handicapped by having to stay behind their rad screens. So they asked us to come to them. Our factor notified the company, the company's interested . . . and that, sirs, is why we're here."

"Mmm. They gave location data for their home system?" Valland asked.

"Apparently so," I said. "Space coordinates, velocity vector, orbital elements and data for each planet of the star."

"Must've been a bitch, transforming from their math to ours."

"Probably. The factor's report gives few details, so I can't be sure. He was in too big a hurry to notify headquarters and send the Yonderfolk back—before the competition heard about them. But he promised we'd soon dispatch an expedition. That's us."

"A private company, instead of an official delegation?" Rorn bridled.

"Oh, come off it," Valland said. "Exactly which government out of a million would you choose to act? This is too damn big a cosmos for anything but individuals to deal with it."

"There'll be others," I said fast. A certain amount of argument on a cruise is good, passes the time and keeps men alert; but you have to head off the kind which can fester. "We couldn't keep the secret for long, even if we wanted to. Meanwhile, we do represent the Universarium of Nordamerik, as well as a commercial interest.

"Now, here are the tapes and data sheets . . . ."

IV

THE SHIP DROVE OUTWARD.

We had a large relative velocity to match. The days crawled past, and Landomar's sun shrank to a star, and still you couldn't see any change in the galaxy. Once we'd shaken down, we had little to do—the mechs operated everything for us. We talked, read, exercised, pursued our various hobbies, threw small parties. Most of us had lived a sufficient number of years in space that we didn't mind the monotony. It's only external, anyhow. After a century or three of life, you have plenty to think about, and a cruise is a good opportunity.

I fretted a little over Yo Rorn. He was always so glum, and apt to be a bit nasty when he spoke. Still, nothing serious developed.

Enver Smeth, our chemist, gave me some concern too. He was barely thirty years old, and had spent twenty-five of them under the warm wing of his parents on Arwy, which is a bucolic patriarchal settlement like Landomar. Then he broke free and went to the space academy on Iron—but that's another tight little existence. I was his first captain and this was his first really long trip. You have to start sometime, though, and he was shaping up well.

Very soon he became Hugh Valland's worshiper. I could see why. Here the boy encountered a big, gusty, tough but good-natured man who'd been everywhere and done everything—and was close to three thousand years old, could speak of nations on Manhome that are like myth to the rest

23

of us, had shipped with none less than Janosek—and to top the deal off, was the kind of balladeer that Smeth only dreamed of being. Valland took the situation well, refrained from exploiting or patronizing, and managed to slip him bits of sound advice.

Then came the Captain's Brawl. In twenty-four hours we would be making the jump. You can't help feeling a certain tension. The custom is good, that the crew have a final blast where almost anything goes.

We ate a gourmet dinner, and made the traditional toasts, and settled down to serious drinking. After a while the saloon roared. Alen Galmer, Chu Bren, Galt Urduga, and, yes, Yo Rorn crouched over a flying pair of dice in one corner. The rest of us stamped out a hooraw dance on the deck, Valland giving us the measure with ringing omnisonor and bawdy words, until the sweat rivered across our skins and even that mummy-ancient line, "Why the deuce aren't you a beautiful woman?" became funny once more.

> "—So let's hope other ladies
> Are just as kind as Alixy,
> For, spaceman, it's your duty
> To populate the galaxy!"

"Yow-ee!" we shouted, grabbed for our glasses, drank deep and breathed hard.

Smeth flung himself onto the same bench as Valland. "Never heard that song before," he panted.

"You will," Valland drawled. "An oldtimer." He paused. "To tell the truth, I made it up myself, 'bout five hundred years back."

"I never knew that," I said. "I believe you, though."

"Sure." Smeth attempted a worldly grin. "With the experience you must've had in those lines by now. Eh, Hugh?"

"Uh . . . well—" The humor departed from Valland. He emptied his goblet with a sudden, almost violent gesture.

Smeth was in a lickerish mood. "Womanizing memories, that's the kind you never edit out," he said.

Valland got up and poured himself a refill.

I recalled that episode at Lute's, and decided I'd better divert the lad from my gunner. "As a matter of fact," I said, "those are among the most dispensable ones you'll have."

"You're joking!" Smeth protested.

"I am not," I said. "The really fine times, the girls you've really cared for, yes, of course you'll keep those. But after a thousand casual romps, the thousand and first is nothing special."

"How about that, Hugh?" Smeth called. "You're the oldest man aboard. Maybe the oldest man alive. What do you say?"

Valland shrugged and returned to us. "The skipper's right," he answered shortly. He sat down and stared at what we couldn't see.

I had to talk lest there be trouble, and wasn't able to think of anything but banalities. "Look, Enver," I told Smeth, "it isn't possible to carry around every experience you'll accumulate in, oh, just a century or two. You'd swamp in the mass of data. It'd be the kind of insanity that there's no cure for. So, every once in a while, you go under the machine, and concentrate on the blocs of memory you've decided you can do without, and those particular RNA molecules are neutralized. But if you aren't careful, you'll make big, personality-destroying gaps. You have to preserve the overall pattern of your past, and the important details. At the same time, you have to be ruthless with some things, or you can saddle yourself with the damnedest complexes. So you do *not* keep trivia. And you do not overemphasize any one type of experience, idea, or what have you. Understand?"

"Maybe," Smeth grumbled. "I think I'll go join the dice game."

Valland continued to sit by himself, drinking hard. I wondered about him. Being a little tired and muzzy, I stayed on the same bench. Abruptly he shook his big frame, leaned over toward me, and said, low under the racket:

"No, skipper, I'm neither impotent nor homosexual. Matter's very simple. I fell in love once for all, when I was young. And she loves me. We're enough for each other. We don't want more. You see?"

He hadn't shown it before, but he was plainly pretty drunk. "I suppose I see," I told him with care. "Wouldn't be honest to claim I feel what you mean."

"Reckon you don't," he said. "Between them, immortality and star travel changed everything. Not necessarily for the worse. I pass no judgments on anybody." He pondered. "Could be," he said, "if I'd stayed on Earth, Mary and I would've grown apart too. Could be. But this wanderin' keeps me, well, fresh. Then I come home and tell her everything that happened."

He picked up his omnisonor again, strummed a few bars, and murmured those lyrics I had heard when first we met.

> *"I'll sing me a song about Mary O'Meara, with stars like*
> *a crown in her hair.*
> *Sing of her memory rangin' before me whatever the ways*
> *that I fare.*
> *My joy is to know she is there."*

Well, I thought with startling originality, *it takes all kinds.*

V

WE WERE ready to jump.

Every system was tuned, every observation and computation finished, every man at his post. I went to the bridge, strapped myself into recoil harness, and watched the clock. Exact timing isn't too important, as far as a ship is concerned; the position error caused by a few minutes' leeway is small compared to the usual error in your figures. But for psychological reasons you'd better stay on schedule. Pushing that button is the loneliest thing a man can do.

I had no premonitions. But it grew almighty quiet in my helmet as I waited. The very act of suiting up reminds you that something could go wrong; that something did go wrong for others you once knew; that our immortality isn't absolute, because sooner or later some chance combination of circumstances is bound to kill you.

What a spaceship captain fears most, as he watches the clock by himself on the bridge, is arriving in the same place as a solid body. Then atoms jam together and the ship goes out in a nuclear explosion. But that's a stupid fear, really. You set your dials for emergence at a goodly distance from the target sun, well off the ecliptic plane. The probability of a rock being just there, just then, is vanishingly small. In point of fact, I told myself, this trip we'd be in an ideal spot. We wouldn't even get the slight radiation dosage that's normal: scarcely any hydrogen for our atoms to interact with, between the galaxies.

Nevertheless, we were going two hundred and thirty thousand light-years away.

And I do not understand the principle of the space jump. Oh, I've studied the math. I can recite the popular version as glibly as the next man: "Astronomers showed that gravitational forces, being weak and propagating at light velocity, were insufficient to account for the cohesion of the universe. A new theory then postulated that space has an intrinsic unity, that every point is equivalent to every other point. One location is distinguished from another only by the n-dimensional coordinates of the mass which is present there. These coordinates describe a configuration of the matter-energy field which can be altered artificially. When this is done, the mass, in effect, makes an instantaneous transition to the corresponding other point in space. Energy being conserved, the mass retains the momentum—with respect to the general background of the galaxies—that it had prior to this transition, plus or minus an amount corresponding to the difference in gravitational potential."

It still sounds like number magic to me.

But a lot of things seem magical. There are primitives who believe that by eating somebody they can acquire that person's virtue. Well, you can train an animal, kill it, extract the RNA from its brain, put this into another animal, and the second beast will exhibit behavior characteristic of that same training.

The clock showed Minute One. I cut the drive. We ran free, weight departed, silence clamped down on me like a hand.

I stared out at the chaotic beauty which flamed to starboard. *So long, galaxy*, I thought. *I'll be seeing you again, in your entirety; only what I'll see is you as you were a quarter of a million years ago.*

The time reeled toward Minute Two. I unfastened the safety lock and laid my gloved finger on the red button.

Nothing came over the comsystem into my earplugs. We were each without words.

Time.

The shock was too horrible. I couldn't react.

No blackness, with the great spiral for background and a wan red star glowing before us. A planet filled the screen.

I saw the vision grow, kilometers per second, hurtling upon us or we upon it. Half was dark, half was mottled with landscape, agleam with waters, under a blood-colored day. No chance to reset the jump unit and escape, no chance to do anything but gape into the face of Death. A roaring filled my helmet. It was my own voice.

Then Hugh Valland's tone cut through, sword-like with what I should have cried. "Pilots! For God's sake, reverse us and *blast!*"

That jarred me loose from my stupor. I looked at the degree scale etched in the screen and the numbers on the radar meters, I made an estimate of vectors and ripped out my commands. The engine boomed. The planet swept around my head. Acceleration stuffed me down into my harness and sat on my chest. Unconsciousness passed in rags before my eyes.

We had too much velocity to kill in what time remained. But we got rid of some of it, in those few minutes before we struck atmosphere; and we didn't flash directly down, we entered at a low angle.

With such speed, we skipped, as a stone is skipped across a river. Shock after shock slammed into us. Metal shrieked. The viewscreens filled with incandescence. This ungainly hulk of a vessel was never meant to land. She was supposed to lie in orbit while our two ferries served her. But now she had to come down!

Somehow, Bren and Galmer operated the pilot board. Somehow they kept the drive going, resisting our plunge, bringing us groundward in a fury that only sufficed to boil away our outer plates. When the main drive was ruined and quit, they used the steering units. When those went out, one by one, they used what was left. Finally nothing remained and we fell. But then we were so low, our speed so checked, that a man had some chance.

I heard the bellowings, the protest and the breaking of steel. I felt the furnace heat from the inner bulkheads, through and through my spacesuit until lips cracked open and nasal passages were tubes of anguish. I saw the water below, and braced myself, and remembered I must not. Relax, float free, let harness and suit and flesh absorb the shock.

We hit.

I crawled back to awareness. My mouth was full of blood, which had smeared my faceplate so that it was hard to see out. One eye being swollen shut didn't help. Hammers beat on every cell of me, and my left arm wouldn't respond. I thought in a dull, vague way, *My skull can't really be split open . . . .*

The men!

Nothing sounded except my own rattling breath. But surely, I cried, this was because the comsystem had been knocked out. *Got to go see. Got to unstrap and find my men.*

I didn't set my teeth against the pain of movement. That would have taken more control than I had, in my present state. I whimpered through the many minutes of fumbling. At last I slid free, onto the canted, buckled deck. I lay there a while before being able to get up and feel my way aft.

The ship was dead. No screens functioned, no ventilators whispered, no lights glowed except the evershine panels spotted along the corridors. By their dim greenishness I stumbled and slipped, calling out names.

After some part of eternity a human shape met me in the passage. Not quite human, a two-legged bulk with a grotesque glassy head; but the radio voice was Hugh Valland's. "That you, skipper?" I clung to him and sobbed.

"We're lucky," he told me. "I've been lookin' us over. If we'd crashed in a sea we'd be done. The whole after section's flooded. We've sunk. But the nose seems to be pokin' out into air."

"How are the others?" I dared ask.

"Can't find anyone in the engine compartment," he said grimly. "I took a flash and went into the water, but no trace, just a big half-melted hole in the side. They must've been carried out with the main reactor. So there's two gone." (Let me record their names here: Morn Krisnan and Roli Blax, good men.) Valland sighed. "Don't seem like young Smeth'll last long either."

Seven men, I thought, *in poor shape, wrecked on a planet that every probability says is lethal for them.*

"I came through fairly well, myself," Valland went on. "Suppose you join the rest. They're in the saloon. I want to gander out of a lock. I'll report to you."

The room where we met was a cave. One evershine, knocked out of its frame, had been brought in for light. It threw huge misshapen shadows across crumpled walls. Snags of girders protruded like stalactites. The men slumped in their armor. I called the roll: Bren, Galmer, Urduga, Rorn. And Smeth, of course. He hadn't left us yet.

He was even conscious, more or less. They had laid him out on a bench as well as might be. I peered into his helmet. The skin looked green in what light we had, and the blood that bubbled from his mouth was black. But the eyeballs showed very white. I tuned up his radio for him and heard the harsh liquidity of his breathing.

Rorn joined me. "He's done," he said without tone. "His harness ripped loose from the stanchions when they gave way, where he was, and he got tossed against a bulkhead. So his ribs are stove through his lungs and the spine's broken."

"How do you know?" I challenged. "His suit's intact, isn't it?"

Teeth gleamed in the murk that was Rorn's face. "Captain," he said, "I helped carry the boy here. We got him to describe how he felt, when he woke, and try to move his arms and legs. Look at him."

"Mother, mother," said the gurgle in my earplugs.

Valland came back. "The ferryboats are smashed too," he said. "Their housin's took the main impact. We won't be leavin' this planet soon."

"What's outside?" I asked.

"We're in a lake. Can't see the oppsite edge. But the waters fairly shallow where we are, and there's a shore about two kilometers off. We can raft to land."

"For what?" Rorn flared.

"Well," Valland said, "I saw some aquatic animals jump. So there's life. Presumably our kind of life, proteins in water solution, though of course I don't expect we could eat it."

He stood a while, brooding in gloom, before he continued: "I think I can guess what happened. You remember the Yonderfolk said their system included a planet in the liquid-water thermal zone. The innermost one, with a mass and density such that surface gravity ought to be two-thirds Earth standard. Which feels about right, eh?"

Only then did I notice. Every motion had hurt so much that nothing except pain had registered. But, yes, I was lighter than before. Maybe that was the reason I could keep my feet.

"The Yonderfolk gave us information on each planet of this star," Valland went on. "I don't know exactly who made the big mistake. There was that language problem; and the the factor on Zara was in a hurry to boot. So my guess is, the Yonderfolk misunderstood him. They thought we wanted to land here first, it bein' more comfortable for us; they even thought we had the means to land directly. So they supplied figures and formulas for doin' just that. And we assumed they were tellin' us how to find a nice, safe, convenient point way off from the sun, and cranked the wrong stuff into our computer."

He spread his hands. "I could be wrong," he said. "Maybe the factor's to blame. Maybe some curdbrain in the home office is. Fact remains, though, doesn't it, that you don't blindly jump toward a point in space—because you have to allow for your target star movin'. You use a formula. We got the wrong one."

"What do we do about it?" Rorn snapped.

"We survive," Valland said.

"Oh? When we don't even know if the air is breathable? We could light a fire, sure, and test for oxygen. But how about other gases? Or spores or— Argh!" Rorn turned his back.

"There is that," Valland admitted.

He swung about and stared down at Smeth. "We have to unsuit him anyway, to see if we've got a chance to help him," he said finally. "And we haven't got time—he hasn't—for riggin' an Earth-atmosphere compartment. So—"

He bent onto one knee, his faceplate close to the boy's. "Enver," he said gently. "You hear me?"

"Yes . . . yes . . . oh, it hurts—" I could scarcely endure listening.

Valland took Smeth's hand. "Can I remove your suit?" he asked.

"I've only had thirty years," Smeth shrieked. "Thirty miserable years! You've had three thousand!"

"Shut up." Valland's tone stayed soft, but I've heard less crack in a bullwhip. "You're a man, aren't you?"

Smeth gasped for seconds before he replied, "Go ahead, Hugh."

Valland got Urduga to help. They took the broken body out of its suit, with as much care as its mother would have given. They fetched cloths and sponged off the blood and bandaged the holes. Smeth did not die till three hours later.

At home, anywhere in civilization—perhaps aboard this ship, if the ship had not been a ruin—we might have saved him. We didn't have a tissue regenerator, but we did have surgical and chemical apparatus. With what we could find in the wreckage, we tried. The memory of our trying is one that I plan to wipe out.

Finally Smeth asked Valland to sing to him. By then we were all unsuited. The air was thin, hot and damp, full of strange odors, and you could hear the lake chuckle in the submerged compartments. Valland got his omnisonor, which had come through unscathed while our biogenic stimulator shattered. "What would you like to hear?" he asked.

"I like . . . that tune . . . about your girl at home."

Valland hesitated barely long enough for me to notice. Then: "Sure," he said. "Such as it is."

I crouched in the crazily tilted and twisted chamber, in shadows, and listened.

"The song shall ride home on the surf of the starlight and leap to the shores of the sky,
Take wing on the wind and the odor of lilies and Mary O'Meara-ward fly.
And whisper your name where you lie."

He got no further than that stanza before Smeth's eyes rolled back and went blind.

We sank the body and prepared to leave. During the past hours, men who were not otherwise occupied had taken inventory and busied themselves. We still had many tools, some weapons, clothes, medicines, abundant freeze-dried rations, a knockdown shelter, any number of useful oddments. Most important, our food unit was intact. That was no coincidence. Not expecting to use it at once on Yonder, nor at all if our stay wasn't prolonged, we had stowed it in the recoil-mounted midsection. With the help of torches run off the capacitors, as long as they lasted, the work gang assembled a pontoon raft. We could ferry our things ashore.

"We'll live," Hugh Valland said.

I gazed out of the lock, across the waters. The sun was low but rising, a huge red ember, one degree and nineteen minutes across, so dull that you could look straight into it. The sky was deep purple. The land lay in eternal twilight, barely visible to human eyes at this distance, an upward-humping blackness against the crimson sheen on the lake. A flight of creatures with leathery wings croaked hoarsely as they passed above us. The air was dank and tropical. Now that my broken arm was stadered, I could use it, but those nerves throbbed.

"I'm not sure I want to," I muttered.

Valland spoke a brisk obscenity. "What's a few years? Shouldn't taken us any longer to find some way off this hell-ball."

I goggled at him. "Do you seriously believe we can?"

He lifted his tawny head with so much arrogance that he wasn't even aware of it, and answered: "Sure. Got to. Mary O'Meara's waitin' for me."

VI

THE SUN crept down almost too slowly to notice. We had days of daylight. But because the night would be similarly long and very dark, we exhausted ourselves getting camp established.

Our site was a small headland, jutting a few meters above the shore and thus fairly dry. Inland the country ran toward a range of low hills. They were covered with trees whose broad leaves were an autumnal riot of bronzes and yellows, as far as we could identify color in this sullen illlumination. The same hues prevailed in those tussocky growths which seemed to correspond to grass, on the open stretch between woods and water, and in the reedy plants along the mud beach. But this was not due to any fall season; the planet had little axial tilt. Photosynthesis under a red dwarf star can't use chlorophyll.

We saw a good deal of wild life; and though the thin air deadened sound, we heard much more, off in the swamps to the north. But having only the chemical apparatus left to make a few primitive tests—which did show certain amino acids, vitamins and so forth missing, as you'd expect—we never ventured to eat local stuff. Instead we lived off packaged supplies until our food plant was producing.

To get that far was our most heartbreaking job. In theory it's quite simple. You fit together your wide, flat tanks, with their pumps and irradiator coils; you sterilize them, fill them with distilled water, add the necessary organics and minerals; you put in your cultures, filter the air intake, seal off the whole thing against environmental contamination, and sit back. Both phyto- and zooplankton multiply explosively till equilibrium is reached. They are gene-tailored to contain, between them, every essential of human nutrition. As needed, you pump out several kilos at a time, return the water, cook, flavor, and eat. (Or you can dispense with flavors if you must; the natural taste is rather like shrimp.) You pass your own wastes back through a processor into the tank so that more plankton can grow. The cycle isn't one hundred percent efficient, of course, but comes surprisingly close. A good construction only needs a few kilos of supplementary material per year, and we had salvaged enough for a century, blessing the Guild law that every spaceship must be equipped fail-safe.

Simple. Sure. When there are machines to do the heavy work, and machines to control quality, and it isn't raining half the time, and you're acclimated to air and temperature, and your nerves aren't stretched wire-thin with looking for the menaces that instinct says must lurk all around, and you don't keep wondering what's the use of the whole dismal struggle. We had to assemble a small nuclear generator to supply current, and level a site for the tanks with hand shovels, and put up our shelter and a stockade, and learn about the planet faster than it could find new ways to kill us, simultaneously.

About hazards: No carnivores attacked. A few times we glimpsed web-arctoid giants. They kept their distance; doubtless we smelled inedible to them and doubtless we were. But a horned thing, thrice the mass of a human, charged from the brush at Rorn and Galmer as they went surveying. They gave it the full blast of two heavy torchguns, and it didn't die and didn't die, it kept on coming till it collapsed a meter away, and then as they left it crawled after them for a long while . . . . Bren almost drowned in a mudhole. The ground was full of them, concealed by plants growing on their surface . . . . Urduga came near a sort of vine, which grabbed him. The sucker mouths couldn't break his skin, but he couldn't get loose either. I had to chop free; naturally we never left camp alone . . . . Though we had portable radios and gyrocompasses, we dreaded losing our way in these featureless marshlands . . . . From time to time we noticed bipedal forms skulk in the distant brush. They disappeared before we could bring optical aids to bear, but Galmer insisted he had glimpsed a spear carried by one of them. And without the main reactor, the ship's heavy weapons were inert. We had a few sidearms, nothing else.

Microbes we simply had to risk. We should be immune to all viruses, and odds were that no native bacteria or protozoa could make headway in our systems either. But you never knew for certain, and sometimes you lay awake wondering if the ache in your body was only weariness. Until we got our hut assembled, endless dim day and frequent rains made sleep hard to come by.

In spite of strain, or perhaps because of it, no quarrels flapped up at first—except once, when I told Bren and Galmer to make measurements. I wanted precise values for gravity, air pressure, humidity, magnetism, ionization, horizon distance, rotation period, solar spectrum lines, whatever could be found with a battery of instruments from the ship.

"Why now?" Rorn demanded. He was no more gaunt and dirty than the rest of us, as we sat in our shelter while another storm drummed on the roof. "We've hardly begun the heavy work like building a stockade."

"Information-gathering is just as urgent," I answered. "The sooner we know what kind of place we're in, the sooner we can lay plans that make sense."

"Why those two men, though?" Rorn's mouth twisted uncontrollably. We hadn't yet installed lights, and the single flash hanging overhead cast his eyes into thick shadow, as if already a skull looked at me. "We can take turns. Easy to sit and twiddle with a pendulum and clock."

"Well," Bren said mildly, "that sounds fair."

"Veto," I said. "You boys are trained in navigation and planetography. You can do the job quicker and better than anyone else."

"Besides," Valland pointed out, "they won't sit continuously. Between sun shots, for instance, we'll put 'em to somethin' real hard." He grinned. "Like maybe findin' some way to make the bloody plankton imitate steak."

"Don't remind me!" Rorn grated. "Aren't we miserable enough?"

"What do you propose to do about our troubles?" I asked sharply. A gust of wind made the thin metal walls shake around us.

"What do *you*? How do we get off of here?"

"The most obvious way," Urduga said, "is to fix a radio transmitter that can beam to Yonder."

"If they use radio," Rorn countered. "We don't any more, except for special things like spacesuits. Why shouldn't they space-jump electron patterns, the same as us? Then they'll never detect our signal—if you actually can build an interplanetary 'caster with your bare hands!"

"Oh, we got tools and parts," Valland said. "Or maybe we can fix one of the ferries. Got to take a close look into that possibility. Simmer down, Yo. Once I get a home brewery rigged, we'll all feel better."

"If you don't want to work with us, Rorn," Urduga added, "you have the freedom of this planet."

"None of that!" I exclaimed. "Once we turn on each other, we're done. How about a song, Hugh?"

"Well, if you can stand it." Valland got his omnisonor and launched into another ballad he had translated from old times on Earth. No doubt it should have been something decorous about home and mother, or something heroically defiant. But

39

our ragged, hungry, sweaty crew got more out of *The Bastard King of England*. Rorn alone didn't laugh and join in the choruses; however, he kept his despair quiet.

Over a period of standard days, Bren and Galmer accumulated quite a bit of information. Though the red sun was still aloft, their photoscreen 'scope could pick out other galaxies for astronomical reference points. Their laser-beam transit and oscilloscope could accurately measure that sun's creep down the sky. In calm weather they had a flat western horizon, out where the lake ran beyond vision. The short year enabled them to take a good sample of our orbit. And so on and so on. When added to what little the Yonderfolk had reported (they'd visited this world in the past, but were really no more interested in it than Earthmen in Sol I), and to general scientific principles, these data enabled us to make a fairly good sketch.

We were in the middle northern latitudes of a planet which had a diameter three percent greater than Earth's. The size was no cause for astonishment. Dim stars haven't enough radiation pressure to inhibit such masses from condensing close to them out of the original dust cloud. Nor were we surprised that weight was only 0.655 standard. The very old systems, formed in early generations, have little in the way of heavy elements like iron. This planet lacked a metallic core, must in fact be sima clear to the center. Hence the low mean specific gravity and the absence of a magnetic field.

Nor did it own any satellites. Solar gravitation had served to prevent that. This force had also, over billions of years, slowed rotation until one hemisphere faced inward. Then tides in water and atmosphere continued to act, until now the globe had a slow retrograde rotation. Combined with a sidereal year of ninety-four and a half Earth-days, this spin gave us a diurnal period of forty-four Earth-days on the surface: three weeks of lights, three weeks of dark.

Coreless, the planet had no vertical tectonic and orogenic

forces worth mentioning. Once the mountains formed by surface distortion had eroded away, no new ones got built. Nor were there great ocean basins. We were lucky to have come down by this wet land; we wouldn't likely find anything much better anywhere, and most of the world must be submerged.

Though the total irradiation received was only slightly less than what Earth gets, it lay heavily in the red and infrared. The sun's wavelength of maximum emission was, in fact, about 6600 ångströms, near the end of the human-visible spectrum. This accounted for the steamy heat we lived with. Scarcely any ultraviolet light was given off, and none of that penetrated to us; we needed artificial irradiation as much as our plankton did. Nor does a red dwarf spit out many energetic charged particles. Accordingly, while the planet was ancient indeed—fifteen billion years at a conservative guess— it still had plenty of water, and an atmosphere corresponding at sea level to a medium-high terrestrial mountaintop.

Given air, a hydrosphere, and an infrared oven in the sky, you don't have to have actinic radiation (what we would call actinic, I mean) for nature's primeval chemicals to become life. It simply takes longer. As we had noted, since we could breathe, there were photosynthetic plants. They probably utilized one of the low-level enzyme-chain processes which have been observed in similar cases within the galaxies. Likewise the animals. In spite of having less energetic biochemistries than we did, they seemed to be just about as active. Shooting and dissecting some, we found elaborate multiple hearts and huge, convoluted lungs, as well as organs whose purposes we couldn't guess. Evolution eventually produces all possible capabilities.

Including intelligence. The sun was touching the lake's rim when Urduga shouted us to him. From camp nobody could make out our ship very well, except through goggles. Those were uncomfortable to wear in this climate. Besides, the cells that powered their infrared conversion and photon multiplication wouldn't last forever. So we left them off as much as possible. Now we slapped them on and stared out at the upward-thrusting nose of the *Meteor*.

There, in a fiery shimmer across the water, were four canoes. Long lean shapes with high prows, they were manned by a good dozen creatures apiece. We could barely see, against that sun-dazzle, that the crews were a little under human size, bipeds, powerfully legged and tailed. We launched our raft and paddled toward them, but they hastened off. Before long they had vanished into dusk.

I, who have met thousands of different races, still feel that each new one is a new epoch. Stars, planets, biological systems fall into categories; minds do not, and you never know what strangeness will confront you. Though this first glimpse of the Herd had so little result, I hate to tell of it casually.

But you can imagine what talking we did afterward in camp.

VII

THIS EVENING the galaxy rose directly after sunset. In spite of its angular diameter, twenty-two degrees along the major axis, our unaided eyes saw it ghostly pale across seventy thousand parsecs. By day it would be invisible. Except for what supergiants we could see as tiny sparks within it, we had no stars at night, and little of that permanent aurora which gives the planets of more active suns a sky-glow. There was some zodiacal light, but that was scant help. We must depend on fluorescents, flashes, fire and goggles to carry on our work.

But then that work reached a crisis point. The generator was operating, the plankton tanks breeding food, the camp snugged down within a stockade of sharpened logs. We'd continued indefinitely manufacturing small comforts and conveniences for ourselves. But the question could no longer be shoved aside: what were we going to do to break free?

Would we? I knew the result if we didn't. When our teeth wore down to the gums, and no biogenic apparatus was on hand to stimulate regrowth, we could make dental plates. When monotony got unendurable, we could build or explore or otherwise occupy ourselves. But when at length there were too many unedited memory bits, we would gradually lose our reason.

Sleep evaded me. The shelter was hot and stank of man. The other cots crowded in on mine. Bren snored. My arm was healing with the speed of immortal flesh and bone, but on occasion still pained me. Finally I rose and walked outside.

The yard lights were off. No use inviting attention during a rest period. Between hut and stockade lay a well of blackness, relieved only by a bluish watery glow where irradiator coils energized our plankton. A wind boomed softly, warm and dank, full of swamp musks; the generator whirred in its shell; distantly came a beast's hoot; lake water lapped among those rustling plants we called reeds.

And I heard another sound: Valland's omnisonor. He was on watch. Tonight he didn't sing, he stroked forth lilting notes that spoke of peace. I groped my way to the crude skeleton tower on which he sat, light switches and a gun ready to hand.

He sensed me. "Who's there?" he called.

"Me. Mind if I come join you for a little?"

"No. Glad of company. Sentry-squat gets a mite lonesome."

I climbed up and sat on the platform's bench beside him. Since I hadn't taken my goggles, he was no more than another big shadow. The sky was clear, except for a few thin clouds reflecting the galaxy's glow. It sheened on the lake, too; but shoreward, night drank down its light and I was blind.

Vast and beautiful, it had barely cleared the horizon, which made it seem yet more huge. I could just trace out the arms, curling from a lambent nucleus . . . yes, there was the coil whence man had come, though if I could see man by these photons he would still be a naked half-ape running the forests of Earth . . . . Otherwise I was only able to see three glitters which we now knew were planets.

"What was that tune you were playing?" I asked.

"Somethin' by Carl Nielsen. Doubt if you've heard of him. He was a composer on Earth, before my time but popular yet when I was young."

"After three millennia, you still remember such details?" I wondered.

"Well, I keep goin' back there, you know, on account of

Mary," Valland said. "And Earth doesn't change much any more. So I get reminded. My later memories are the ones I can dispense with."

I realized that this must the reason he, with his abilities, was not commanding a ship. That would have had him star-hopping at somebody else's orders. I didn't know when I'd see Lute and Wenli again, for instance, if I got back into space. The company rotated personnel among home stations, so fifty years was an entirely possible gap. Valland must return home a good deal oftener.

"She seems to be quite a girl, yours," I said.

"Oh, yes," he whispered into the wind.

"You're married?"

"No official contract." Valland laughed. "Plain to see, skipper, you're post-exodus. Mary'd follow the old custom and take my name if—" He broke off.

"You know," I said, for I wanted to speak of such things in this foreign night, "you've never shown us her picture. And everybody else practically carries an album of his women around with him."

"I don't need any stereo animation," he said curtly. "Got a better one in my head." Relaxing, he laughed once more. "Besides, she said once—this was when breeks had hip pockets—she said it didn't seem like a very sentimental gesture, carryin' her picture next to my"—he paused—"heart."

"You've got me curious, though. Dog my hatch for me if I'm prying, but what does she look like?"

"Shucks, I'm only too glad to talk about her. Trouble is, words're such feeble little quacks. That's why I made me a song. Adapted from an old Swedish one, to be honest."

"Swedish? I don't recall any planet named Swede."

"No, no, Sweden, Sverige, a country, back when Earth had countries. Nice people there, if a bit broody. I'm part Swede myself."

Valland fell silent. The galaxy glimmered so coldly above the lake that I had to say something. "What about Mary?"

"Oh." He started. "Yes. Well, she's tall, and has a sort of rangy walk, and laughs a lot, and her hair catches the sunlight so— No, sorry, words just won't fit her."

"Well, I'd like to meet the lady," I said, "if we reach Earth."

"We will," Valland answered. "Somehow." His arm rose, pointing, a massive bar across the clouds. "That planet there, orange color. Must be Yonder. We don't need to go any further than that."

"Two hundred and thirty thousand light-years in no time," I said bitterly, "and a few million kilometers are too much for us."

"Well, it's a big universe," he said. "We don't shrink it any by crossin' it."

After a moment he added: "We can make Yonder, though. The more I think and look at what's available to us, the more I'm convinced that between two wrecked ferries and parts of a wrecked ship, we can put together one sound vessel. No use wishin' we could do anything with the space jump apparatus. That's so much scrap, and we'd never fix it even if we knew how. So we won't be sendin' the Yonderfolk any signals that way."

"Frankly, I'm skeptical about our chances of simply building an interplanetary maser," I confessed.

"Oh, we'll do that, kind of incidentally," Valland said. "Same as we'll make conspicuous marks in the territory around here, in case somebody comes flyin' by. But Yo was right, a while back. They aren't likely to have the right kind of radio receivers on Yonder. And as for a rescue party, well, at best it'll be an almighty long time before anybody figures out what could've happened to us, and I'll make book that nobody does. Not with so scanty and confused a record to go on.

"So . . . I figure our sole decent chance is to flit to Yonder in person. We needn't build a very fancy spaceboat, you realize. A one-man job for a one-way trip, with no special radiation screenin' required. I've checked. Been an engineer myself, several kinds of engineer, now and then, so I know. One powerplant is almost intact. Repairman's data in the microfiles aboard ship amount to a complete set of plans, which we can modify for our particular purposes. What machine tools we don't now have, we can repair, or build from scratch.

"Sure, sure, a long, tough job. The precision aspects, like assemblin' control panels or adjustin' drive units, they'll be worse than any sheer labor. But we can do it, given patience."

"Hold on," I objected. "The brute force problem alone is too much for us. Six men can't juggle tons of metal around with their muscles. We'll need cranes and—and make your own list. We'll have to start this project down near the bottom of shipyard technology.

"Hugh, we haven't got enough man-years. If we don't go memory-crazy first, we'll still be making bedplates when the supplementary chemicals for the food tanks give out. And I refuse to believe we can do anything about *that*."

"Probably not," Valland admitted. "I never claimed we could start a whole biomolecular industry. But you're overlookin' somethin', skipper. True, half a dozen men make too small a labor force to build a spaceship, even by cannibalizin', in the time we have. However— Hey!"

He sprang to his feet.

"What is it?" I cried.

"Shhh. Somethin' out there. Approaching' real slow and careful. But two-legged, and carryin' things. Let's not scare 'em off. Valland stepped to the ladder and handed me his goggles. "Here, you stay put. Cover me as well as you can, but don't switch on any lights. Our kind of light may well hurt their eyes. I'll kindle a torch to see by. They must know fire."

I stared and stared into murk. Shadow shapes in shadow land . . . . "Looks as if they're armed," I muttered.

" 'Course they are. Wouldn't you be? But I doubt they'll slip a pigsticker into me on no provocation." Valland laughed, most softly but like a boy. "You know," he said, "I was just speakin' of the devil, and what came by? A bigger pair of horns than Othello thought he had!"

I didn't follow his mythological references, but his meaning was plain. My own heart jumped inside me.

There is an old game in which you show a picture of a nonhuman to your friends and ask them to describe the being. No xenological coordinates allowed; they must use words alone. The inexperienced player always falls back on analogy. Like Valland, simply to be jocular, remarking that the Azkashi resembled web-footed kangaroos, a bit shorter than men, with hands and hairless gray skins, bulldog muzzles, mule ears, and eyes as big as the Round Tower. Which means nothing to that ninety-nine percent of the human race who have never been on Earth and have never heard of animals many of which are extinct anyway.

Myself, I think the game is silly. I'd be satisfied to speak of bipeds adapted to a world mostly swamp and water. I would mention the great yellow eyes, which saw only a short way into those frequencies we call red and otherwise had to focus infrared waves—largely because they could also see fairly well at night. I might say the beings didn't have nostrils, but closable slits beneath the ears, since this gave their voices an odd snarling quality. The barrel chests were also significant, betokening a metabolism that required more oxygen per breath than we who are blessed with iron-based hemoglobin. It is certainly worth recording that the species was bisexual, viviparous, and homeothermic, though not technically mammalian.

In general, though, I don't care what image you develop. What matters about a people is technology, thought, art, the whole pattern of life.

As for technics, the score of hunters who entered our compound were high-level paleolithic. Their weapons were spears, tomahawks, daggers, and blowguns. Stone, bone and wood were beautifully worked and tastefully ornamented. They went nude except for a sort of leather harness, which supported a pouch as well as tools and armament. But an older one who seemed to be their leader had a representation of the galaxy tattooed on his head.

We were relieved to find no obviously alien semantics. These people would be much easier to understand than the Yonderfolk—or so we thought. For example, they had individual names, and their gestures were the kind humans would make in attempting sign language. When we fetched gifts—a steel knife for ya-Kela the boss and some bits of plastic and other junk for his followers—they yelped and danced with delight. They had brought presents of their own, local handicrafts, which we accepted with due dignity. There came an embarrassing moment, several hours later, when three Azkashi who had slipped out into the woods returned with a big game animal for us. We were doubtless expected to eat it, and had no idea if it would poison us. But Valland carried the situation off by soaking the body in camp fuel and setting it alight on a heap of wood. Our visitors got the idea at once: this was how the strangers who indicated they had come from the galaxy accepted an offering.

"In fact," Valland remarked to me, "they're smart fellows. They must've watched us from the woods for a long time before decidin' to send a delegation. My guess is they waited for the galaxy to rise; it's a god or whatnot to them, and then they felt safer against our *mana*. But now that they're here

49

and know we don't mean any harm, they're tryin' hard for communication."

Ya-Kela was, at least, and so was Valland. Most of the other hunters left after a while, to take word back home. Man and nonman squatted in the compound, by firelight, drew pictures and exchanged gestures. Rorn complained about the darkness outside our hut. I overruled him. "We've seen them cover their eyes against our normal illumination," I said. "We don't want them to go away. They may be our labor force."

"Indeed?" Rorn said. "How'll you pay them?"

"With metal. I don't know how many thousands of knives and saws and planes we can make out of scrap from the ship, and you must have noticed how ya-Kela appreciates the blade we gave him. I saw him holding it up once and singing to it."

"Nice theory. Only . . . captain, I've dealt with primitives too. Generally they don't make proper helpers for a civilized man. They don't have the drive, persistence, orderliness, not even the capability of learning."

"Rather like your caveman ancestors, huh, Yo?" Urduga gibed.

Rorn flushed. "All right, call it a culture pattern if you want. It's still real."

"Maybe it isn't in this case," I said. "We'll find out."

With a good bit more hope in me, I started organizing us for work. First we had to jury-rig a better lighting system aboard the *Meteor*, so we could operate effectively. Next, with spacesuits doubling as diving rigs, we must patch most of the holes in the hull, seal off the remaining compartments, pump out the water and float her ashore. Then there'd be the construction of a drydock, or whatever we decided was best. Then we must take a complete inventory, so we'd know exactly what was possible for us to build; and lay concrete plans; and— The list looked infinite. But we had to begin somewhere. By burning torch and electric flare, we rafted out to the wreck.

Valland stayed behind, dealing with ya-Kela. That didn't look very strenuous, and again Rorn protested. "I don't give a belch if it's fair or not," I threw back at him. "Somebody has to spend full time learning the language, and Hugh's got more talent for that sort of thing than any two of you clump-feet put together."

Which was true. With the help of his omnisonor for noises that the human throat would not form, he could soon produce every Azkashi phoneme; and then it was not so much lin-guistics as a sense of poetry that was needed to fit them into meaningful phrases.

I was not too surprised when, after several Earth-days, he told me that ya-Kela and the others wanted to go home—taking him along. He was eager to make a visit. What could I do but agree?

VIII

With a woodsranger's wariness, ya-Kela reserved judgment. Perhaps he had misunderstood those few words and gestures the stranger called ya-Valland could make. Perhaps ya-Valland did not really claim to be the emissary of God.

For surely he had curious weaknesses. He was as night blind as any downdevil once he took off his fish-resembling mask. Without tail or footwebs, he stumbled awkward through the marshes; and whenever the party swam across a body of water, he was still more clumsy and soon grew tired. Besides, he must push those things he carried on his back a-head of him, lashed to a log. One could accept that he did not speak the speech of the Pack—God must use a tongue more noble—but he was ignorant of the simplest matters, must actually be restrained from walking into a dart bush. There might be some magical reason for his not touching ordinary food and, instead, opening little packets of powder and mixing them with water to swell the bulk before he cooked himself a meal. But why must he send the water itself steaming through a thing of bottles joined by a tube, rather than lap up a drink on his way?

Ya-Eltokh, one of the four who had remained to accompany them back, growled, "He is weirder than any of the Herd. And that great thing he came in, sitting out in Lake Silence! How sure are you that he is not some downdevil animal sent to trap us?"

"If so, the Herd has been clever," ya-Kela said, "for our watchers told how their canoes fled when the strangers tried

52

to come near. And you know well that prisoners we tortured were made to confess that the downdevils did not appear to have anything to do with that which, generations ago, came from the sky. Why, then, should the enemy have brought this new manifestation about?" He signed the air. "I am the One of the Pack. The thought was mine that we should seek the strangers out, for they might be from God. If I was wrong, it is my souls that will suffer; but with this hand I will plunge the first spear into ya-Valland."

He hoped that would not come to pass. The big ugly creature was so likable in his fashion, and the music he made was somehow more important than the sharp blade he had given. He explained, after much fumbling on both sides, that the tune he made most often was a song to his she. But when he heard those notes, little ghosts ran up and down the skin of ya-Kela. There was strong magic in that song.

They continued to seek understanding whenever they camped. Ya-Valland guided the lessons with marvelous skill. By the time they reached the lairs, he could do a little real talking.

It was good to be back in hill country. The Herd fighters seldom ventured into this land of long ridges and darkling valleys, noisy rivers and silent woods. Ya-Kela snuffed a wind that bore the odor of ninla nests, heard the remote scream of a kurakh on the prowl, saw God swirl radiant above Cragdale, and bayed to call his folk. They slipped from dells and thickets until the trail was a stream of lithe, padding hunters, and went together to the caves where the Pack dwelt.

Ya-Kela took ya-Valland into his own place. His aunt, su-Kulka, made the guest welcome and prepared a bed. His she and youngs were frightened and kept in the background, but that was as it should be anyhow. Now ya-Kela settled down to toil with the newcomer as he might have settled down to chasing a onehorn till it dropped. And as God mounted yet

higher in heaven, serious talk became possible. It went halt-
ingly, with many misunderstandings; but it went.

The great question was hardest to pose and get answered.
Ya-Valland seemed to make an honest effort, but his words
contradicted each other. Yes, he was from God. No, he was
not of God . . . . Finally he swung to asking questions himself. Ya-Kela replied, in the hope of making himself clear
when his turn came again.

"God is the Begetter, the One of the World. All others are
less than Him. We pray to God alone, as He has commanded,"
ya-Kela said, pointing and acting. He returned from the cave
mouth and squatted against his tail once more. The fire was
big, throwing the painted walls into lurid smoky relief. But it
didn't appear to make much light for ya-Valland.

"The downdevils are the enemies of God. They deny Him,
as does the Herd which serves them. But we know we are
right to course for God: because He does not rule our lives.
He asks only worship and upright conduct of us. Furthermore, He lights the night for us, on those times when He is
risen after sunset. And then the downdevils can see but
poorly." Mutter: "Almost as poorly as you, my friend-?-
enemy." Aloud: "Such of the Herd as we have captured
when they came raiding say the downdevils made the world
and rule it. And true, they have powerful things to give. But
the price is freedom."

"The Herd people are like you, then?" ya-Valland asked.

"Yes and no. Many of them resemble us, and we have
learned over generations that certain Azkashi whom Herd
raiders take prisoner are used for breeding stock. But others
look most unlike any member of this Pack or any other Pack,
and none of them think like us. They are afraid of God, even
when the sun is in the sky at the same time to hide Him; and
they worship the downdevils."

That much conversation took the entire while between two
sleeps. Then ya-Kela must judge disputes among his folk;

54

for he was the One. Meanwhile ya-Valland studied language with su-Kulka, su-Iss, and other wise old shes.

Thus he was better able to explain himself at the following talk: "We fell from the sky, where our own Pack hunts. We cannot return until we have fixed our boat. That will be the work of many years, and cannot be done without many hands. For this we will pay in goods, blades such as we gave you, tools that will lighten your labor, perhaps also teaching of arts you do not know yourselves."

"But how shall the Pack be fed meanwhile?" ya-Kela asked.

"Given the use of certain weapons we own, fewer hunters can bring in ample game. Besides, they will soon drive off those enemies who trouble you."

Now this I may doubt, ya-Kela thought. *You showed us your thunderous arms back at your camp. But are they really more potent than the downdevils'? I do not know. Perhaps you do not either.*

He said merely, "That is good; yet such is not the ancient way. When you go, and leave a large number of our youngs who have not had time to learn the skills we live by, what then?"

"You're one hell of a bright boy, you know?" said ya-Valland in his own speech. He replied, "We must consider that also. If we plan well, there need be no hungry years; for the tools and weapons you earn will keep you fed until the old ways are learned afresh. Or it is even possible—though this I cannot promise—that my people will wish to come and trade with yours."

He leaned forward, his eyes brilliant in the firelight, the musicmaker in his lap talking sweetly as God Himself. "We must begin in a small way in any case, ya-Kela. Find me only a few clever young hes that are willing to come back with me and work for knives like yours. Then, in the course of a year or so, we will find out if this is good for our two sides."

"Gr-r-um." Ya-Kela rubbed his muzzle thoughtfully. "You utter no ill word there. But let me think on the matter before I say anything to the Pack at large."

That period, shortly before sleep, ya-Valland spoke into a little box he carried. It answered him, as had often happened before. But this time ya-Kela saw him grow tense, and his voice was chipped sharp and his smell became acrid.

"What is wrong?" asked the One, with hand on knife.

Ya-Valland bit his lip. "I may as well tell you," he said. "I know you still keep watchers, who will send word here as soon as they can reach the drums. Vessels have landed by the camp of my people, and some from the crews have entered the stockade to talk."

"The Herd does not use the laguage of the Pack," ya-Kela said. Dampness sprang forth on his skin. "Some have learned it, true. But none of your folk save you have mastered any but a few shards of Azkashi. How can there be talk?"

Ya-Valland was silent for a long while. The waning fire spat a few flames. That light picked out the shes and youngs, crouched frightened in the inner cave.

"I do not know," ya-Valland said. "But best I return at once. Will you give me a guide?"

Ya-Kela sprang to the cave mouth and bayed after help. "You lie!" he snarled. "I can tell that you hold something back. So you shall not leave before we have the entire truth from your downdevil mouth."

Ya-Valland could not have followed every word. But he rose himself, huge and strange, and clasped the weapon that hung at his belt.

IX

WE ALWAYS left one man on the guard tower while the rest were at the ship. What Valland had radioed—good thing our gear included some portables!—suggested that attack by certain rivals of the Azkashi was not unthinkable. He hadn't learned much about them yet, except that they belonged to quite a different culture and must have sent those canoes we'd spied at sunset.

No doubt the Azkashi were prejudiced. They were . . . well, you couldn't call them simple hunters and gatherers. A Pack was only vaguely equivalent to a human-type tribe; Valland suspected that rather subtler concepts were involved. He was still unsure about so elementary a matter as what "Azkashi" meant. It referred collectively to the different Packs, which shared out the inland hunting grounds and lakeside fishing rights, spoke a common tongue and maintained a common way of life. But should the name be translated "hill people" as he thought at first, or "free people," or "people of the galaxy god," or what? Maybe it meant all those things, and more.

But at any rate, the Shkil, as ya-Kela called them, sometimes preyed on the Azkashi; and in the past, they had driven the Packs out of lands on the far side of Lake Silence. This, and certain other details which Valland got during his struggle for comprehension, suggested a more advanced society, agricultural, spreading at the expense of the savages. Which in turn made me wonder if the Shkil might not be potentially more useful to us. On the other hand, they might be hostile,

57

for any of a multitude of reasons. We took no chances. A man in the tower, with gun and searchlights, could hold off an assault and cover the landing of his friends.

By chance, I was the sentry when the Shkil arrived. The galaxy was hidden in a slow, hot rain; my optical equipment could show me nothing beyond the vapors that steamed under our walls. So I had to huddle cursing beneath an inadequate roof while they maddened me with snatches of radioed information from the spaceship. Finally, though, the data were clear. A large band of autochthones had appeared in several outsize canoes and a double-hulled galley. They wanted to confer. And . . . at least one of them spoke the Yonderfolk language!

I dared not let myself believe that the Yonderfolk still maintained an outpost on this planet, so useless and lethal to them. But I felt almost dizzy as I agreed that two or three of the newcomers might enter our compound along with the returning work party. And when they came, destruction take thoughts of treachery, we left no one on the tower. We settled for barring the gate before we led our guests into the hut.

Then I stood, soaked, hearing the rain rumble on our roof, crowded with my men between these narrow walls, and looked upon wonder.

Our visitors were three. One resembled the Azkashi we had already met, though he wore a white robe of vegetable fiber and a tall white hat, carried a crookheaded staff like some ancient bishop, and need but breathe a syllable for the others to jump at his command. One was a giant, a good 240 centimeters in height. His legs and arms were disproportionately long and powerful, his head small. He wore a corselet of scaly leather and carried a rawhide shield; but at our insistence he had left his weapons behind. The third, by way of contrast, was a dwarf, also robed, but in gray. He kept his eyes shut and I took a while to realize that he was blind.

The one with the staff waved his free hand around quite coolly, as if extraplanetary maroons were an everyday affair. "*Niao*," he said. I gathered this was his people's name for themselves. He pointed to his own breast. "Gianyi."

"Felip Argens," I said, not to be outdone. I introduced my comrades and summed them up: "Men."

"We've told him that much," Urduga murmured in my ear. "He stood in the prow of that galley and talked for—you know how long. But you're better at the Yonder lingo than any of us, captain."

I ought to be. I'd studied, as well as electro-crammed, what little had been learned on Zara. Not that we could be sure the language was what the Yonderfolk used among themselves. It might well be an artificial code, like many others I had met, designed for establishing quick communication with anyone whose mind wasn't hopelessly alien. No matter. Gianyi of the Niao had also mastered it.

"Sit down, everybody," I babbled. "What can we offer them? Better not anything to eat or drink. Presents. Find some good presents, somebody. And for mercy's sake, whisky!"

We had a little guzzling alcohol left. It steadied me. I forgot the rain and the heat and the darkness outside, bending myself to talk with Gianyi.

That wasn't any light job. Neither of us had a large vocabulary in that language of gestures as well as sounds. What we had in common was still less. Furthermore, his people's acquaintance with it antedated mine by many generations, and had not been reinforced by subsequent contact. You might say he had another dialect. Finally, a language originated by beings unlike his race or mine was now filtered through two different body types and cultural patterns—indeed, through different instincts; I had yet to discover how very different.

So I can no more set down coherent discourse for Gianyi

and me than I could for ya-Kela and Valland. I can merely pretend:

"We came from the sky," I said. "We are friendly, but we have been wrecked and need help before we can leave. You have met others, not akin to us but also from the sky, not so?"

"They tell me such beings came," Gianyi said. "It was before my time, and far away."

That made sense. In an early stage of space travel, the Yonderfolk would have visited their neighbor planets. Finding intelligent life here, they would have instituted a base from which to conduct scientific studies—before they discovered the space jump and abandoned this world for ones more interesting and hospitable to them. And it would have been an unlikely coincidence if that base happened to have been anywhere near here.

How, though, had the mutual language been preserved through Earth centuries after they left? And how had it traveled across hundreds or thousands of kilometers to us? I asked Gianyi and got no good answer through the linguistic haze. The Ai Chun could do such things, he tried to explain. The Ai Chun had sent his party to us, making him the commander since he was among those Niao who were traditionally instructed in sky-talk. He bowed his head whenever he spoke that name. So did the blind dwarf. The giant remained motionless, poised; only his eyes never rested.

"A ruling class," Bren suggested to me. "Theocrats?"

"Maybe," I said. "I have an impression they're something more, though." To Gianyi: "We will be glad to meet the Ai Chun and make gifts to them as well as to the rest of your people."

He got unreasonably excited. I must not lump Niao and Ai Chun together. That was wrong. That was bad medicine. I apologized for my ignorance.

Gianyi calmed down. "You will meet the Ai Chun," he said. "You will come with us to them."

"Well, one or two of us will," I agreed. We had to take some risks.

"No, no. Every one of you. They have so ordered."

Not being sure whether that last term indicated a fiat or simply a request, I tried to explain that we could not abandon our camp. Gianyi barked at the giant, who growled and took a stiff-legged step forward. I heard guns leave their holsters at my back.

"Easy! Easy!" I sprang to my feet. "You want to start a war?" Gianyi rose also and waved his bully boy back. We faced each other, he and I, while the rain came down louder. The dwarf had never stirred.

I cleared my throat. "You must know that those from the sky have great powers," I said. "Or if you do not, the Ai Chun should. We have no wish to fight. We will, however, if you insist we do what is impossible. Have all the Niao come here? Certainly not. Likewise, all of us cannot go away with you. But we will be glad to send one or two, in friendship."

When I had made this clear, which took time, Gianyi turned to the dwarf and spoke a while in his own high-pitched language. Something like pain went across the blind countenance. The answer was almost too low to hear. Gianyi folded his hands and bent nearly to the floor before he straightened and addressed me again.

"So be it," he told me. "We will take a pair of you. We will leave two canoes here to keep watch. The crews can catch fish to live. You are not to molest them."

"What the bloody blazes is going on?" Urduga whispered behind me.

I looked at the dwarf, who was now shivering, and made no replay. That poor little thing couldn't be the real chief of the party. Well, I've met different kinds of telepathic sensitives among the million known civilizations; none like him, but—

"Think it's a good idea to go, captain?" Galmer asked.

"I don't think we have much choice," I told him, trying hard to keep my voice steady. Inside, I was afraid. "We'll be here a long time. We've got to know what we're up against."

"They may mean well in spite of their manners," Bren said.

"Sure," I said. "They may." The rain gurgled as it fell onto soaked earth.

While Gianyi and his escort waited impassively, we discussed procedure. Our representatives were to be taken to the opposite shore, where the Niao had a frontier settlement. From Valland's questioning of ya-Kela, we knew the lake was broad, an inland sea. Still, we should get across in a couple of standard days, given those swift-looking boats. We might or might not be able to maintain radio contact. Valland could, but he hadn't traveled so far. Under the tenuous ionosphere of this planet, we needed a hypersensitive receiver to read him.

I must go, having the best command of Yonder. An extra man was desirable, both as a backup for me—the situation looked trickier than Valland's—and as evidence of good faith on our part. Everyone volunteered (who could do otherwise, with the rest of us watching him?) and I picked Yo Rorn. He wasn't my ideal of a traveling companion, but his special skills could be duplicated by Valland and Bren working in concert, whereas nobody but Urduga could fix a drive unit and Galmer was alone in knowing the ins and outs of a control system.

We started to pack our gear, more or less what Valland himself had taken along. Bedrolls; plastic tent; cooking and distilling utensils; lyophilized food from stores; medical kit; torchguns and charges; radio, extra capacitors, hand-cranked minigenerator for reviving them; flashes, goggles, photoplates, space garments— The receiver buzzed. I thrust across the crowded hut and sat down. "Hello?" I shouted.

"Me here," Valland's voice said, tiny out of the speaker. "Just reportin'. Things look pretty hopeful at this end. How's with you?"

I told him.

He whistled. "Looks like the Herd's found you out."

"The what?"

"The Shkil. You remember. I've about decided it translates best as 'Herd.' What'd you say they call themselves?"

"The Niao. With somebody else in charge that they name as Ai Chun."

"Um. The downdevils, I suppose. My own translation again, of an Azkashi word that means somethin' like 'the evil ones in the depths.' Only I thought the downdevils were a set of pagan gods, as contrasted with the local religion where the galaxy's the one solitary original God, beware of imitations."

Valland's lightness was not matched by his tone. I realized with a jolt that this was putting him in a bad fix. What with the strain of the past hours, trying to unravel Gianyi's intent, we'd forgotten that our shipmate was among people who hated and feared those I was to depart with.

And . . . surely the Pack had watchers by the edge of wilderness.

"We can hardly avoid going," I said, "but we'll stall till you can return here."

"Well, I'll try. Hang on a bit."

There followed some ugly noises.

"Hugh!" I cried. "Hugh, are you there?"

The rain had stopped, and silence grew thick in the hut. Gianyi muttered through the dwarf to his unknown masters. I sat and cursed.

Finally, breathlessly, Valland said:

"Matters peaked in an awful hurry. Ya-Kela figured treachery. He called in his goons and wanted to put me to the question, as I believe the polite term is. I pointed out that I could shoot my way clear. He said I'd have to sleep eventually and then he'd get me. I said no, I'd start right back to camp if need be, might not make it but I'd sure give him a run for his money. Only look, old pal, I said, let's be reasonable. My people don't know anything about the downdevils. Maybe they've been tricked. If so, I'll want your help to rescue them, and between us we can strike a hefty blow. Or suppose the worst, suppose my people decide to collaborate with the enemy because they offer a better deal. Then I'll be worth more to you as a hostage than a corpse. I got him calmed down. Now he wants to lecture me at length about how bad the downdevils are."

"Try to explain the idea of neutrality," I said. "Uh, Hugh, are you sure you'll be all right?"

"No," he said. "Are you sure for yourself?"

I tried to answer, but my throat tightened up on me.

"We're both in a bad spot," Valland said, "and I wouldn't be surprised but what yours is worse. Ya-Kela swore by his God he won't hurt me as long as I keep my nose clean. I won't be a prisoner, exactly; more like a guest who isn't permitted to leave. I think he'll stand by that. I've already handed him my gun, and still he's lettin' me finish before he sequestrates the radio. So I ought to be safe for the time bein'. You go ahead and sound out the whosits—Ai Chun. You've got to. Once you're back, we'll parley."

I tried to imagine what it had been like, standing in a cave full of wolves and surrendering one's only weapon on the strength of a promise. I couldn't.

X

THE GALLEY walked fast over the water. Except for creak and splash of oars, soft thutter of a coxswain's drum, an occasional low-voiced command, it was too silent for my liking. Torches lit the deck built across the twin hulls. But when Rorn and I stood at the rail, we looked into murk. Even with goggles, we saw only the galaxy and its wave-splintered glade; the accompanying canoes were too far out.

Rorn's gaunt features were shadow and flicker beside me. "We're facing something more powerful than you maybe realize," he said.

I rested my hand on my gun butt. Its knurls comforted me. "How so?" I asked.

"Those boats which first came, and ran away. They must have been from the place we're headed for now. What's its name again?"

"Prasiyo, I think."

"Well, obviously they simply chanced on us, in the course of fishing or whatever. The crews were ordinary unspecialized Niao, we saw that. But they didn't take the responsibility of meeting us. No, they reported straight back to Prasiyo. Now normally, you know, given a generally human-type instinct pattern, a technological-geographical situation like this one makes for individualism."

I nodded. Tyranny gets unstable when a cheap boat can pace a warship and there's a wilderness for dissatisfied people to vanish into. The Niao had not fled us because of timidity. Their harrying of the Azkashi proved otherwise. So the Niao must *like* being subservient.

"Nevertheless," Rorn continued, "it took some while before this delegation arrived. That means it had to be organized. Authorized. Which means word had to get back to a distant front office."

"Now that needn't take long, given telepathy."

"My exact point. The masters therefore debated the matter at length and took their time preparing to contact us. There's also the business of the Yonder language having been preserved so long and carried so far. What these clues point to is: we're on the marches of a very big and very old empire."

I was surprised. Rorn hadn't seemed capable of reasoning so clearly. "Makes a good working hypothesis, anyhow," I said. "Well, if we can get them to help us, fine. They'll have more resources, more skills of the kind we need, than the Pack does. Of course, first we have to get Hugh back into camp with us."

Rorn spat.

"You don't like him, do you?" I asked.

"No. A loudmouthed oaf."

"He's your crewfellow," I reminded him.

"Yes, yes. I know. But if matters should come to a pass—if we can only save ourselves, the whole remaining lot of us, by abandoning him—it won't weigh on my conscience."

"How would you like to be on the receiving end of that philosophy?" I snapped. "We orbit or crash together!"

Rorn was taken aback. "I didn't mean—Captain, please don't think I—"

Ghostlike in his robes and hat, Gianyi glided to me. "I have thought you might be shown the ship," he offered.

We were both relieved at the interruption, as well as interested in a tour, and followed him around the deck. The cabin assigned us was pretty bare. The others, for Gianyi and three more Niao of similar rank, were a curious blend of austere furnishing with ornate painted and carved decoration. I noticed that two symbols recurred. One was a complicated knot, the other a sort of double swastika with a circle super-imposed. I asked about them.

Gianyi bowed deep. "The knot is the emblem of the Ai Chun," he said.

"And this?"

He traced a sign on his breast. "The *miaicho* bound fast by the power of the solar disc."

A few minutes later, I observed that helmsmen and look-outs wore broad hats with that second insigne on them. I asked why. Gianyi said it was protection against the miaicho.

Rorn was quick to understand. He pointed at the immense spiral in heaven. "That?"

"Yes," Gianyi said. "Its banefulness is great when there is no sun at the same time. We would not have crossed the water tonight had the Ai Chun not commanded."

So, I thought, the God of the Azkashi was some kind of demon to the Niao. Just as the Niao's venerated Ai Chun were the downdevils of the Pack. . . .

Gianyi made haste to take us below. The hull, like everything else, was well built. No metal anywhere, of course; ribs and planks were glued, then clinched with wooden pegs. Construction must have been a major job. Gianyi admitted there was just this one ship on the lake; otherwise only canoes were needed, to fish and to keep the savages in their place. But whole fleets plied the oceans, he said. I was prepared to be-lieve him after he showed me some very fine objects, cera-mic and plastic as well as polished stone.

The crew intrigued me most. The rowers worked in sev-eral shifts on a well ventilated, lantern-lit deck. They were all of a kind, with short legs, grotesquely big arms and shoulders, mere stumps of tail. Some fighters were on board too, like the colossus I had already seen. To our questions, Gianyi replied that other types of Niao existed, such as divers and paddy workers. He himself belonged to the intel-lectual stock.

"You may only breed within your own sort?" I asked.

"There is no law needed," Gianyi said. "Who would wish to mate with one so different, or keep alive a young which was not a good specimen? Unless, of course, the Ai Chun command it. They sometimes desire hybrids. But that is for the good of all the Niao."

When I had unraveled that this was what he had actually said, and explained to Rorn, my companion reflected in our own tongue: "The system appears to operate smoothly. But that has to be because hundreds, thousands of generations of selective breeding lie behind it. Who enforced that, in the early days?" I saw him shudder. "And how?"

I had no reply. There are races with so much instinct of communality that eugenics is ancient in their cultures. But it's never worked long enough at a time for others, like the human race, to be significant. You get too much individual rebellion; eventually some of the rebels get power to modify the setup, or wreck it.

So perhaps the autochthones of this planet did not have human-type minds after all?

No—because then how did you account for the Azkashi?

In spite of the temperature, we felt cold. And belowdecks was a cavern, full of glooms, lit by no more than a rare flickering lamp. We excused ourselves and returned to our little room. It had only one sconce, but we stuck spare candles in their wax around us.

Rorn sat down on his bedroll, knees hugged to chin, and stared at me where I stood. "I don't like this," he said.

"The situation's peculiar," I agreed, "but not necessarily sinister. Remember, the Yonderfolk suggested we might base ourselves here."

"They supposed we'd arrive with full equipment. Instead, we're helpless."

I regarded him closely. He was shivering. And he had been so competent hitherto. "Don't panic," I warned him. "Remember, the worst thing that can happen to us is no more than death."

"I'm not sure. I've been thinking and—well, consider. The Ai Chun, whoever they are, haven't much physical technology, for lack of metal. But they've gone far in biology and mentalistics. Consider their routine use of telepathy, which to this day is too unreliable for humans. Consider how they could regulate the Niao, generation after generation, until submissiveness was built into the chromosomes. Could they do the same to us?"

"A foul notion." I wet my lips. "But we have to take our chances."

"Harder for me than you."

"How so?"

He looked up. His features were drawn tight. "I'll tell you. I don't want to, but you've got to understand I'm not a coward. It's only that I know how terrible interference with the mind can be, and you don't."

I sat down beside him and waited. He drew a breath and said, fast and flat, eyes directly to the front:

"Faulty memory editing. That's not supposed to be possible, but it was in my case. I was out in the Frontier Beta region. A new planet, with a new med center. They didn't yet know that the pollen there has certain psychodrug properties. I went under the machine, started concentrating as usual, and . . . and I lost control. The technicians didn't see at once that something was wrong. By the time they did, and stopped the process— Well, I hadn't lost everything. But what I had left was unrelated fragments insufficient for a real personality. Worse, in a way, than total amnesia. Yet I couldn't bring myself to wipe the slate clean. That would be like suicide."

"How long ago was this?" I asked when he stopped to gulp for air.

"Forty-odd years. I've managed to . . . to restructure myself. But the universe has never felt quite right. A great many very ordinary things still have a nightmare quality to them, and—" He beat the deck with his fist. "Can you imagine going through something like that again?"

"I'm terribly sorry," I said.

He straightened. His aloofness came back to him. "I doubt that, captain. People have to be far closer than we are to feel anything but a mild regret at each other's troubles. Or so I've observed. I spend a lot of time observing. Now I don't want to talk further about this, and if you tell anyone else I'll kill you. But take my advice and watch your mind!"

XI

WE CAME to Prasiyo in darkness, and left in darkness, so to
me it was only torches, shadows, sad strange noise of a horn
blown somewhere out in the night. Afterward I saw it by
day, and others like it; and as I became able to ask more
intelligent questions, the Niao I met could give me better
answers. Thus I learned a great deal, and never in my traveling have I met a society more outlandish.

But that's for the xenological files. Here I'll just say that
Prasiyo wasn't a town, in the sense of a community where
beings lived in some kind of mutual-interest relationship, with
some feeling of common tradition. Prasiyo was only a name
for that lakefront area where the docks happened to be. This
made it convenient to locate certain workshops nearby. So
the igloo-shaped huts of the Niao clustered a bit thereabouts—
unlike in the wide, wet agricultural region that stretched behind Lake Silence, on and on to the ocean. Yes, and still
further, because there were Niao who had been bred for
pelagiculture too.

The Pack maintained a true community, in those lairs where
Valland was now a prisoner. Later we found that there were
other savages, in other wild parts of the world, who did likewise. Some of them had progressed to building little villages.
But the Niao, who appeared to be civilized, had nothing of
the kind anywhere. For they were the Herd, and herds don't
create nations.

Neither do gods.

Our galley didn't go to the wharf. Instead, we moored

alongside a structure built some distance offshore: a square, massive stone pile that loomed over us in the night like a thundercloud. Lanterns picked out soldier Niao guarding the ramparts. Helmeted and corseleted, armed with knives, pikes, bows, catapults, they stood as if they were also stone. Gianyi and three fellow scribes conducted us off ship, in a stillness so deep that the gangplank seemed to drum beneath our feet. The blind dwarf scuttled after us. They all bent low in reverence to the gate.

"What is this?" I asked.

"The house that is kept for the Ai Chun, when they choose to visit us here," Gianyi said mutedly. "You are honored. No less than two of them have come to see you."

I had a last glimpse of the galaxy before we entered. The sight had always appeared unhuman to me before—lovely, but big and remote and indifferent. Now it was the one comfort I had.

Lamps burned dim down the wet, echoing length of a hall. There was no ornament, no furniture, only the great gray blocks. We passed through an archway into a room. It was too broad and feebly lit for me to see the end, although I had my goggles on. Most of the floor was occupied by a pool. I conjectured rightly that this place must connect with the lake by submarine passages.

The downdevils lay in the water.

A physical description would sound like any amphibious race. They were pinnipeds of a sort, about twice the length and several times the bulk of men. The sleek heads were notable chiefly for the eyes: not so large as those of the bipeds, a very beautiful luminous chalcedony in color. Evolution had modified the spine so that they could sit up when on land. And I suppose the front limbs had developed digits from internal bones: because what I saw was a flipper with four clumsy fingers.

The sea doesn't often bring forth intelligence. But under

special circumstances it can happen. The dolphins of Earth were a famous example. If they had gained the ability to go ashore, to travel cross country in however awkward a fashion, who knows what they might have become? I think the environmental challenge that brought forth the Ai Chun occurred billions of years ago. As the planet lost hydrosphere—which happened slowly indeed, under so chill a sun; but remember how old this world was—more and more dry land emerged. With so many ages behind it, the life that then, step by step, took possession, was not modified fish as on Earth. It was life already air-breathing, with high metabolism and well-developed nervous system. New conditions stimulated further development—you don't need hard radiation for mutation to occur; thermal quantum processes will do the same less rapidly. At last the Ai Chun came into being.

I think too that there was once a satellite, large and close, which lit the nights until finally the sun's field, intense at this short remove, perturbed it away. Or maybe the Ai Chun evolved when the planet had a permanent dayside. For their eyes weren't well adapted to the long nights they now faced. They had substituted firelight for the optic evolution that had taken place in younger species. Perhaps this is the reason they hated and feared the galaxy. In the day sky it was invisible to them, but on alternate nights it ruled the darkness.

All that is for the paleontologists to decide. And it happened so long ago that the evidence may have vanished.

What mattered to Yo Rorn and me, confronting those two beings, was their words. They did not deign to speak directly. They would have had trouble using the Yonder language anyway. The dwarf opened his mouth, moved his arms, and said:

"Through this creature we address you, as we have already observed you from afar. You are kin to those which dwelt here for a space, numerous years ago, claiming to be from above, correct?"

"There is no blood relationship," I said. My heartbeat knocked in my ears. "But you and we and they, like the Niao and the hill people, are thinking animals. I believe this is more important than our bodily shapes."

Gianyi made an appalled hiss. "Have you forgotten whom you speak to?" he cried.

"No offense intended," I said, wondering what local custom I'd violated. "Since you have followed our discussions with your . . . your servants, you know we are ignorant and need help. In exchange we offer friendship as well as material rewards."

"Say further," commanded the Ai Chun.

They drew me out with some extremely shrewd questions. They had forgotten little of what the Yonderfolk had evidently told them. I explained our background, I spoke of the galaxy, its size and distance, the millions of worlds and the powerful races which inhabited them— Why did the scribes, the will-less dwarf himself, cringe?

Sweat glistened on Rorn's skin. "You're telling them the wrong things," he said.

"I know," I answered. "But what's the right thing?" I dropped hand to gun—started to, but my arm wouldn't obey. It was as if the muscles had gone to sleep. With a curse, I focused myself on the task. My hand moved, jerkily, to clasp the butt.

Rallying nerve, I said: "Are you trying to control me? That is no friendly act. And you can't, you see. Our minds are too unlike."

A part of me thought they must also have tried this on the Yonderfolk, and failed so completely against brains based on hydrogen and ammonia that the attempt wasn't noticed. Otherwise we'd have been warned. Then the Ai Chun dissembled, hid their real nature like the hidden part of an iceberg, gave the impression of being harmless primitives. A telpathic folk with a unified, planet-wide culture could do that.

In our case, they didn't bother. They knew far too well that no one would avenge us. The dwarf's monotone said:

"We dismissed the former visitors, and we shall not let you run free in the world. Have no fear. Your potential usefulness is admitted. While you obey, you shall not be harmed. And when you grow old you will be cared for like any aged, faithful Niao."

Rorn and I moved until we stood back to back. The scribes edged off into a dark corner. One downdevil raised himself higher, so that the lamplight gleamed on him. The dwarf spoke:

"We have pondered what reason we might have had in the beginning to bring forth creatures like you and those others. Where we do not supervise it, life on shore often develops in curious ways. Perhaps you do not yourselves know your ancestral history. However, you are ordered at least to desist from telling falsehoods. For we believe now that your existence is not accidental but intended."

Rorn whimpered. "They're in my mind. I can feel them, they're in my mind."

"Shut up and keep ready to shoot," I told him.

I felt it myself, if "felt" is the right word. Unbidden images, impulses, bursts of terror and anger and bliss and lust, a stiffness in my body, my clothes drenched and stinking with perspiration. But the impressions were not intense—about like a mild drunkenness, as far as their power to handicap me went. I told myself, over and over: *These beasts are projecting energies of a type that've been known to our scientists for hundreds of years. They want to stimulate corresponding patterns in my brain. But I belong to another species. My neurones don't work like theirs. I won't give them a chance to find out how I do work. And remember always, in spite of the horror stories, nobody can be "taken over" who keeps his wits about him. It's physically impossible. You're closer to your own nervous system, and better integrated with it, than anyone else can be.*

I clamped my teeth for a moment, then started asking questions.

Abruptly the disturbances in my head stopped. Maybe simply because of the contrast, I felt more in possession of myself than ever before in my life. So for hours I stood talking. All the while, Rorn was silent at my back.

The downdevils responded to me with cold candor. No use trying to reproduce our discussion as such. I don't remember the details. And naturally our conference was often interrupted by explanations of some new term, by arguments, by cogitation until a meaning became clear. They didn't press me, these two in the pool. They weren't in the habit of hurrying. Besides, I slowly saw, they were quite fascinated. They didn't hate us any more than we would hate a pair of wild beasts we had captured for study and possible taming.

At least, there was no conscious hatred. Down underneath, I don't know. We threatened their whole existence.

You see, they were gods.

It was not just that their Niao worshiped them. I doubt the Niao did, anyway, in the human-like sense in which you could say the Azkashi worshiped the galaxy. The Niao were devoted to the Ai Chun as a dog is to a man; they'd been bred for that trait; but aside from a few gestures of respect, they didn't conduct ceremonies. For that matter, the Ai Chun had no religion, if you mean by that a belief in a superior power.

No, they simply thought this was the only world, the whole universe, and they had created it.

The idea was not crazy. Their planet showed few phenomena to inspire awe, like stars or volcanoes or seasons. The Ai Chun had existed in their present form for over a billion years, I imagine. Their natural enemies were exterminated before their recorded history began. In spite of much empirical knowledge, they had never developed a true science. They did not quarrel with each other, they parceled out the world and refrained from overbreeding. One generation lived exactly like the next. Their culture was sufficiently complex that intelligence didn't atrophy; but change was so slow that there remained vast land areas they had not so much as explored. Only lately had their minions been pushing into the Lake Silence region—and not in any pioneer rush, but by calculated degrees. Theirs was a static world.

Individual Ai Chun suffered accidents, grew old, died. That didn't matter. They believed in reincarnation. So it was reasonable to imagine that at some time in the past, in earlier lives, they themselves had made the universe. It was an obvious analogy to the building and stockbreeding they now practiced. Likewise, they knew they made occasional mistakes in their present lives—which accounted for unruly elements in the cosmos.

Besides, had they not, within historical times, added a thinking race to the world?

They had. I saw no reason to doubt their claim. Being poorly adapted to dry land, they domesticated a promising bipedal animal and spent half a million or so Earth-years breeding it for intelligence and dexterity. That was the last great advance their frozen society had made. Now the Niao did for them what they were not able to do for themselves.

Of course, intelligence is a tricky thing. And without techniques of molecular biology, you can never get every wild gene out of a stock. Certain Niao, here and there on the planet, for one reason or another, had gone masterless into new territories. There the demands of an independent life had quickly winnowed out submissiveness. An instinct of devotion remained, making for religion and mutual loyalty. The end result was the Azkashi and other cultures—feral.

The Ai Chun were not alarmed. They thought in million-year terms. They didn't let their Niao expand fast: that could have introduced upsetting factors. Bit by bit, as agricultural acreage increased, the savages would be whittled away. Meanwhile they posed no real threat.

The Yonderfolk, and now we, did. Not that we desired this wretched planet for ouselves. But our very attitude was an insult. Our claim to be from other worlds in an unimaginably big and complicated universe ran into the teeth of a mythology that was old while the dinosaurs still lived. Our machines, our weapons, something as simple as a steel knife, had not been dreamed of here and could not even be copied. By existing, we doomed this whole culture.

The Yonderfolk hadn't stayed long enough to do more than shake the Ai Chun. What they had taught was preserved and brooded on. Now we were here, still another race. But this time the intruders were few and vulnerable. If we could be subjugated, that would prove we were inferior. Then the Ai Chun could assure themselves that outsiders like us had also been created by them in the distant past, for the purpose of inventing things which we would now offer to our gods.

I argued. I tried to show them the pathetic, ridiculous futility of their scheme. I said we couldn't possibly give them more iron than there was in our ship; and if we built them plants to extract light metals, they could still make only the most limited use of the stuff; and if our people should decide to base on this planet, there wouldn't be one damned thing the Ai Chun could do about it; and if they cooperated with us we could offer them infinitely greater rewards— Useless. Such concepts didn't lie within their horizon.

Yet they were neither stupid nor mad. Only different from us.

"The seed we planted long ago is bearing its fruit," said the voice of the dwarf. "We will occupy your camp and put you to work."

"Like fury you will!" I drew my gun. Their minds didn't try to stop me.

I fired a beam into the air. The Niao wailed and covered their eyes. The Ai Chun dived. "You see?" I shouted. "We can kill you and every one of your folk. We can seize a boat and sail back. Our friends will not open their gates to you, and their own weapons will burn you at a distance. We do not want to fight, but if we must, then it is you who will be dead!"

A hand closed on my wrist. An arm locked around mine. The gun clattered free. I stumbled from a push. Whirling, I saw Yo Rorn.

His own gun was out, aimed straight at me. "Hold still," he said.

"What the chaos!" I lurched toward him.

"Stop. I'd hate to burn you down." He spoke quietly. Haloed by darkness, his face was altogether serene. "You've lost," he said.

XII

THE GALAXY was high in heaven when we started back, and
first glimmers of dawn paled it. I still needed my goggles to
see; they showed me Lake Silence ice-gray and ruffled by a
light wind. Rain clouds grew in the north. The air had turned
cold. I stood on the galley deck, looking across to the score of
canoes which escorted us, and again felt horror at how quietly
the Niao worked.

Down below decks, the two Ai Chun rested in a tank of
water. They were going to make a personal inspection after
our camp was occupied. Through their sensitives they were in
touch with their fellows around the globe. Not only this little
fleet was moving against my crew; a planet was.

"No," Rorn said, "they didn't get inside me and pull any
strings. I'm doing what I want to do."

I couldn't look straight into the nirvana of his eyes. The
downdevils were clever, I thought. Sensing his weakness, they
had left me alone, holding my attention with talk, while
through hours they studied him. Not that they had battered
down any defenses he had. He would have known, then, and
appealed for my armed help. But they had watched his re-
actions as one subtle impulse after another was tried. In the
end, they had understood him so well that they had been able
to—to what?

I asked him.

"It was a stroke of luck for them that you took me with you
instead of someone else," Rorn said impersonally. "They
couldn't have operated on a well-developed personality.
They've admitted to me it's not possible to tame even a cap-

tured savage through mentalistics; he has to be broken first by physical means. And we humans are less kin to them than any Azkashi. But in my case, I didn't have much ego strength. I was a bundle of uncoordinated impulses and poorly understood memories. Galactic civilization had little to offer me."

"What did they give you?"

"Wholeness. I can belong here."

"As a nice, safe slave?"

"You don't get any closer to the truth with swear words. I was shown something great, calm, beautiful, at peace with itself. Then they took it away. I got the idea: they'd give it back to me if I joined them."

"So you stopped being human," I said.

"No doubt. What was the use of staying human? Oh, in a hundred years or so I'd have crystallized into your pattern again. But it's a poor one at best, compared to what I have *now*."

I didn't believe he had acted quite freely. Once the Ai Chun got past his feeble resistance, they could explore the neuronic flows until they learned how to stimulate his pleasure center directly. (I wouldn't have allowed them that far in; no normal man would, at least not before techniques like sensory deprivation had made us disintegrate.) But there was no point in telling Rorn that.

Defeat tasted sour in my mouth. "Why do you bother explaining to me?" I asked.

"They told me I should. They want your cooperation, you see."

I made a last attempt. "Try to think," I said. "Your reasoning ability can't be too much impaired yet."

"On the contrary," he smiled, "you wouldn't believe what a difference it makes, not to be insecure and obsessed any longer."

"So think, blast you! I won't remind you of what the rest of

81

us want to get back to, everything from friends and families to a decent yellow sunlight. You've dropped those hopes. But you'll live here for centuries, piling up data that can't be removed, till you go mindless."

"No. They can help me better than any machine."

"They're not supernatural! They can't do everything—can't do a fraction of what we can—why, we've personally outlived a dozen of them, end to end."

"So I've told them. They say it makes us still more valuable. They're not jealous, being reborn themselves."

"You don't believe that guff. Do you?"

"A symbolic truth doesn't have to be a scientific truth. As a race, at least, they're more ancient than we dayflies can imagine."

"But . . . but even in psychology, mentalistics—they're primitive. They don't speak directly to you, mind to mind, do they?" He shook his head. "I thought not," I went on. "There are human adepts back home who could. If that's what you need, you can get it better from them."

"I tried them once. No good. Not the same as here."

"No," I said bleakly, "at home you weren't offered any return to a womb. You weren't presented with any self-appointed gods. You weren't tinkered with. Human therapists only tried to help you be your own man."

His blandness was not moved. "Evidently I didn't want that, down inside," he answered. "Please understand. I don't bear you ill will. In fact, I love you. I love everything in the universe. I could never do that before." He broke off for a moment, then finished in a flat voice: "This is being explained to you so that you'll see you're beaten and won't do anything foolish that might get you hurt. We humans have an important role to play in this world."

He turned and walked off.

My radio had been confiscated, of course. Rorn used his own set to call ahead. His message was exactly what our men hoped for. The Niao were a civilized people who would be glad to supply us with workers in exchange for what we could teach. The brief stay of the Yonderfolk had wakened an appetite for progress in them. I was remaining behind for the time being to arrange details, and treated like an emperor. The Azkashi could easily be persuaded to release Valland. Rorn was bringing the first work gang—a large one, for the initial heavy labor of salvage.

When the wild edge of Lake Silence hove in view, I was taken below. Tied to an upright, I heard snatches of what went on in the following hours. The first exuberant hails, back and forth; the landing; the opened gates; the peaceful behavior, until all possible suspicions were lulled; the signal, and the seizure of each man by three or four Niao who had quietly moved within grabbing distance of him. I heard the Ai Chun wallow past my prison, bound ashore. I sat in darkness and heard the rain begin.

At last a soldier came to unfasten me. I shouldered my pack and went ahead of him, down a Jacob's ladder to a canoe, through a lashing blindness of rain and wind to the beach. Day had now come, tinting the driven spears of water as if with blood. My goggles were blinkered with storm; I shoved them onto my forehead and squinted through red murk. I couldn't see our spaceship. The headland where our compound stood was a dim bulk on my left. No one was visible except my giant guard and the half dozen canoe paddlers. We started off. My boots squelched in mud.

Well, I thought, hope wasn't absolutely dead. After a while, getting no report from us, our company would send another expedition. Presumably that crew would take less for granted than we had, and avoid shipwreck. In time, a human base might be founded on this planet. They might eventually learn about us, or deduce the truth after seeing things we'd been forced to make for the Ai Chun.

Only the downdevils, with Rorn to advise them, would

have provided against that somehow. And would probably, after we had gotten their projects organized for them, take time off to give us a good brainwashing and shape us all into Rorns.

I stumbled. The guard nudged me with a hard thumb.

Rage exploded. I wheeled about, yanked his knife from the sheath, and slashed. The flint blade was keen as any steel. It laid open the burly arm that grabbed at me. Yellow blood spouted under a yellow flare of lightning.

The guard roared. I broke into a run. He came after me. His webbed feet did not sink in the mud like mine and his strides were monstrous. He overhauled me and made a snatch. I dodged. His tail swung and knocked me off my feet.

Rain slapped me in the eyes. He towered above me, impossibly huge. I saw him bend to yank me up again. He kept on bending. His legs buckled. He went down on his belly beside me, trying to staunch the arterial flow with his good hand. His hearts, necessarily pumping more strongly than mine which had hemoglobin to help, drained him in a few seconds.

The boat crew milled closer. They could have taken me. But they had been bred into peacefulness. I reeled erect and stabbed the air with the knife I still held. They flinched away. I ran from them.

A glance behind revealed that one dashed off to report. The rest trailed me at a distance. I made inland. Thunder bawled in my ears. Rain hissed before the wind. My pack dragged me and the breath began to hurt my throat.

The Niao would not leave me. They kept yelping so that when the soldiers had been alerted they could find us. I was no woodsman, least of all on a strange planet. I belonged out among the clean stars that I'd never see again. There was not one chance of my shaking pursuit, not even in the thickest part of the woods that now loomed before me.

I glanced down at my stone knife. There was a release. I stuck it in my belt and kept going.

The forest closed about me. My cosmos was leaves, trunks, withes that slapped my face, vines that caught at my ankles, as I plowed through muck. My eyes were nearly useless here. Swamp rottenness choked my nostrils. I heard some wild animal scream.

It was following me. No . . . those were Niao voices . . . they wailed. A lupine baying resounded in answer. I stopped to pant. In a moment's astounded clarity I knew that of course the Pack had kept a suspicious watch on us. Beneath every fury and fear, I must have remembered and hoped—

When the Azkashi surrounded me I could just see them, four who looked saurian in the gloom. Their weapons were free and the rain hadn't yet washed off every trace of the butchery they had done.

I summoned my few words of their language and gasped, "We go. Shkil come. Go . . . ya-Valland."

"Yes," said one of them. "Swiftly."

Their pace was unmerciful. I've only the haziest recollection of that trip into the hills. Memory ends with a red sun in a purple sky, well over the crags and treetops that surround the lairs. Hugh Valland meets me. He's kept himself and his outfit clean, but hasn't depilated in some while. His beard is thick, Sol golden, and he stands taller than a god. "Welcome, skipper!" his call rings to me. "Come on, let's get you washed and give you a doss and some chow. Lord, you look like Satan with a hangover." I fall into his arms.

I woke on a bed of boughs and skins, within a painted cave. A native female brought me a bowl of soup made from my rations. She howled out the entrance, and presently Valland came in.

"How're you doin'?" he asked.

"Alive," I grunted.

"Yeah," he said, "I can imagine. Stiff, sore, and starved. But you aren't in serious shape, far's I can see, and we've got a lot of talkin' to do." He propped me in a sitting position and gave me a stimulo from his medikit. Some strength flowed into me, with an odd, detached clearness of thought.

I looked past Valland's cross-legged form, through the cave obscurity to the mouth. There was considerable stir outside. Armed males kept trotting back and forth; the smoke of campfires drifted in to me; I heard the barks and growls of a multitude.

"S'pose you tell me exactly what happened," Valland said.

After I finished, he uttered one low whistle of surprise. "Didn't think the downdevils had *that* much goin' for them." He extracted his pipe, stuffed and kindled it, while he scowled.

"We haven't got much time," he said. "I'm damn near out of tobacco."

"I'm more concerned about food," I said. "I remember what you took along and what I was carrying. Between us, we might last till sundown."

"Uh-huh. I was tryin' to put the idea in a more genteel way." He puffed for a bit. "The drums sent word ahead to us here, about the Herd enterin' our camp and then about you bein' on your way to us. That last was the best thing you could possibly have done, skipper. Ya-Kela couldn't have protected me for long if the Pack figured my people had sold out. As was, I got Rorn on the radio. He was pretty frank about havin' taken over on behalf of the downdevils, once he knew I knew you'd run off. He said I should try to escape from here, and he'd send a troop to meet me. I told him where he could billet his troop, and we haven't talked since. My guess was he'd turned coat out of sheer funk. I didn't realize what'd actually happened to him. The poor fool."

Hopelessness welled beneath the drug in me. "What can we do except die?" I asked.

"Hadn't you any notions when you cut out?"

"Nothing special. To die like a free man, maybe."

Valland snorted. "Don't be romantic. You haven't got the face for it. The object of the game is to stay alive, and get back our people and our stuff. Mary O'Meara's waitin' on Earth."

That last sentence was the soft one, but something about it yanked me upright in my bed. *God of Creation*, I thought, *can a woman have that much power to give a man?*

"Relax," Valland said. "We can't do anything right now."

"I gather . . . you've been busy, though," I said.

"Sure have. I stopped bein' a prisoner the minute ya-Kela got across to the Pack that my folk were now also down-devil victims. He'd been ready to trust me anyhow, for some while."

Afterward, when I knew more Azkashi, I was told that Valland had been along on a hunt in which a twyhorn charged past a line of spearmen and knocked down the One. Before the animal could gore him, Valland had bulldogged it. Coming from a higher gravity was helpful, of course, but I doubt that many men could have done the same.

"The problem's been to convince 'em we aren't helpless," Valland said. "They still have trouble believin' that. Throughout their past, they've won some skirmishes with the Herd, but lost the wars. I had an ace to play, however. The Herd's crossed the lake, I said. They'll build an outpost around our ship. Then, to support that outpost, they'll call in their loggers and farmers. If you don't wipe 'em out now, I said, you'll lose these huntin' grounds too." He blew a dragon puff of smoke. "We got the other Packs to agree in principle that everybody should get together and attack this thing while it's small."

"Stone Age savages against energy guns?" I protested.

"Well, not all that bad. I've done soldierin' now and then, here and there, so I can predict a few things. Rorn can't put guns in any other human hands. He'll demonstrate their use to the Herd soldiers. But you know what lousy shots they'll be, with so little practice. Cortez had good modern weapons too, for his time, and men a lot better disciplined than the Aztecs;. but when they got riled enough, they threw him out of Mexico." Thoughtfully: "He made a come-back later, with the whole Spanish power behind him. We have to prevent that."

"What do you propose to do?"

"Right now," Valland said, "I'm still tryin' to hammer into the local heads some notion of unified command and action under doctrine. Fightin' looks easy by comparison."

"But—Hugh, listen, the Packs may outnumber the Herd detachment, but they'll have to charge across open ground. I don't care how poorly laid an energy barrage is, they can't survive. Not to mention arrows. Those Herd archers are good."

"So who says we'll charge?" Valland countered. "For our main operation, anyhow. I've got a plan. It should take the downdevils by surprise. Everything you've told me fits in with what ya-Kela knows, and it all goes to show they can't read minds. If they could, they wouldn't need to transmit words through those midget sensitives. The downdevils read Rorn's emotional pattern, all right, and shifted it for him. But that was done on a basic, almost glandular level. They couldn't've known what he was thinkin', nor what we think."

"Our men are hostages," I reminded him. "Not to speak of our food tanks and the other equipment we need for sur-vival."

"I haven't forgotten." His tone was mild and implacable. "We'll have to take chances, for the men as well as ourselves. Because what have they really got to lose? If we get in fast—"

A shadow darkened the cave mouth. As he joined us, I recognized ya-Kela. He hailed me with the courtesy that most savages throughout the universe seem to use, before he turned to Valland. I couldn't follow his report, but he sounded worried.

Valland nodded. " 'Scuse me," he said. "Business."

"What?" I asked.

"Oh, one of those silly things that're always comin' up. Some Pack chiefs decided they don't like my ideas. If cut-and-run guerrilla fightin' by little independent gangs was good enough for granddaddy, it's good enough for them, and to hell with this foreign nonsense about unity and assigned missions. Ya-Kela can't talk sense into them. I'll have to. If we let anyone go home, pretty soon everybody will."

"Do you think you can stop them?" I fretted, for I knew something about pride and politics myself.

"I been doin' it, since we started this project. Now get some rest. You'll need your strength soon." Valland left with ya-Kela. He had to stoop to get out.

I lay there, cursing my weakness that would not let me go too. Noises came to me, shouts, yelps, snarls. There was the sound of a scuffle; Valland told me later that he had had to underline a logical point with his fist. But presently I heard notes like bugle and drum. I heard a human voice lifted in song, and I remembered some of those songs, ancient as they were, *Starbuck* and *La Marseillaise* and *The March of the Thousand*, forged by a race more warlike than any on this world; then he set his instrument to bagpipe skirls and the hair stood up on my spine. The Packs howled. They didn't comprehend the language, they hardly grasped the idea of an army, but they recognized strong magic and they would follow as long as the magician lived.

XIII

WE CAME DOWN to the shore well south of our objective. By then time was short for Valland and me: little remained of our powdered food. And what had gone on with our people these Earth-days of their captivity? Nevertheless we had to wait on the weather.

That didn't take long, though, on this planet. Rain was succeeded by fog. The Packs divided themselves. A very small contingent went with Valland, a larger one with me; the bulk of them trailed through the woods, ya-Kela at their head.

I was in charge of the waterborne operation, ya-Kela my lieutenant. He was also my interpreter, being among the few who could understand my pidgin Azkashi; for I had no omnisonor to help. And as far as the crews were concerned, he was the commander; I didn't have Valland's prestige either. But this was the key to our whole strategy. The Packs kept dugouts by the lake. They had never used them for anything but fishing. How could it be expected that they would assault what amounted to a navy?

We glided through clouds that were chill and damp, red-gray like campfire smoke. Nearly blind, I could only crouch in the bow of my hollow log while six paddles drove me forward. The Azkashi saw better, well enough to maintain direction and formation. But even they were enclosed in a few meters of sight. And so were our enemies.

I am no warrior. I hate bloodletting, and my guts knot at the thought that soon they may be pierced. Yet in that hour of passage I wasn't much afraid. Better to die in combat than starve to death. I dwelt on the people and places I loved. Time went slowly, but at the end it was as if no time had passed at all.

"We are there," ya-Eltokh breathed in my ear. "I see the thing ahead."

"Back water, then," I ordered unnecessarily; for my watch said we were in advance of the chosen moment. The waiting that followed was hard. We couldn't be sure that some boat-load of impulsive hunters would not jump the gun and give us away. With a fortress to take, we depended on synchrony as well as on surprise. When the minute came, I screamed my command.

We shot forward. The spaceship appeared before me, vast and wetly shimmering in the mist. Two canoes lay at the ladder we had built to the above-water airlock. Their pad-dlers shrieked and fled as we emerged.

I grabbed a rung. Ya-Eltokh pushed ahead of me, up to the open entrance. A Herd soldier thrust down with a spear. Blowguns sighed at my back. The giant yelled, toppled, and splashed into the lake. Ya-Eltokh bounded inside. His toma-hawk thudded.

My mates boiled after him, forcing the doorway. I came last. Our crew had to be first, for only I could guide our party through the ship. But my knowledge made me too precious to spend in grabbing a toehold.

I got into battle aplenty, though. Three of the Pack were down, ripped by soldiers who had come pounding at the alarm. Ya-Eltokh dodged, slashing with his ax at two huge shapes. One of them spied me and charged. Valland had had something new made for me, a crossbow. I had already cocked it. I pulled the trigger and the bolt slammed home. The corridor boomed with his fall.

Then more of our people were aboard. They formed a living wall around me. I cocked and fired as fast as I was able. It wasn't much help, but I did down a couple of worker Niao who had joined the fray. Ax, knife and spear raged around us. Howling echoed from metal.

We needed only hold fast for some minutes, till an overwhelming force of hunters had boarded. There weren't any guards on the ship; no one had looked for this maneuver of ours. When the last of them fell, the workers threw down the tools they had been using for weapons. I tried to stop my people from massacring them, but too much ancient grudge had to be paid off.

Ya-Eltokh came to me, his feet painted with blood. "I see the big boat now," he rasped.

"Don't let it near, but don't let our boats attack it either," I ordered. With fifty or so Azkashi to help, and a single doorway to defend, he shouldn't have a problem. I led a small troop to the lower decks, where we had commenced salvage operations before the Niao arrived.

That job was not any further along. The Ai Chun had no interest in a spaceship as such. Their gangs had been stripping away metal for more prosaic uses.

But Urduga was there, hastily bound when the fight started. I cut him loose and he wept for joy.

"How've you been?" I asked.

"Bad," he told me. "They haven't mistreated us yet, in a physical sense, I mean. We're still being . . . explored, so they'll know exactly what they want to do with us. But I'd gotten to the point where I begged them to send me out here as a supervisor." He looked around with haunted eyes. "So far I've managed to keep them from damaging anything essential."

"We've got to be quick," I said. "The plan is that we draw most of their strength out on the lake. Then our shore force hits them. But Hugh's boys have to take the compound before the enemy thinks to wreck our survival equipment. What can we improvise here against a warship?"

Yes—his *men*.

Combat did not last long after that. At such close quarters the Herd was slaughtered. Never mind the details. What followed was all that mattered. I have to piece it together. But this was when we lost everything we thought we had gained.

Valland broke through the remnants of the fight and led a few Azkashi toward our shack. The door was locked. His fist made the walls tremble. "Open up in there!"

Rorn's voice reached him faintly: "Be careful. I have Bren and Galmer here, and my own gun. I can kill them."

Valland stood for a space. His followers growled and hefted their weapons. Unease was coming upon them like the fog that roiled past their eyes.

"Let's talk," Valland said at length. "I don't want to hurt you, Yo."

"Nor I you. If I let you in, can we hold an honest parley?"

"Sure."

"Wait a minute, then." Standing in red wet murk that was still cloven by the yells and thuds of combat, Valland heard some sounds of the Yonder language. A treble fluting responded.

His Azkashi heard too. A kind of moan went among them, they shuffled backward and ya-Kela exclaimed shakenly: "That is one of the dwarfs. I know how they talk. Our scouts did not see that any of *them* had landed here." He gripped Valland's arm with bruising force. "Did you know, and not tell us?"

As a matter of fact, the human must have thought, *yes*. He had not his omnisonor with him, to aid in shaping tones, but he managed to convey scorn. "Do you fear the down-devils even when they are beaten?"

"They are not like the Shkil. They do not die."

"We may find otherwise." Somehow Valland made them stay put until the colloquy inside ended and the door creaked open.

The blind telepath stood there. Blackness gaped behind him. Rorn's order rasped from within: "You come by yourself, Valland." As the gunner trod through, the dwarf closed the door again.

Rorn activated the lights enough for him to see. Bren and Galmer lay on two bunks, tied hand and foot. A pair of soldier Niao flanked a great wooden tub filled with water. They crouched tense, spears poised, lips drawn back from teeth. Rorn stood before the tank. His energy pistol was aimed at Valland's midriff. His features were also drawn tight; but—maybe just because he had put on a little weight —serenity remained beneath.

Valland glanced at his comrades. "How're you doin', boys?" he asked softly.

"All right," Galmer said.

Bren spat. "Hugh, don't let this cockroach use us against you. It'd be worth getting shot by him, as long as we know you'll squash him later."

Rorn smiled, without noticeable malice, and reminded: "You'll never build your escape vessel if you lose their skills, Hugh. And there's no other way off this planet. The Yonderfolk left nothing behind except a few items the Ai Chun took apart centuries ago. What I've learned while we were here convinces me the Yonderfolk really don't use radio for communication, nor are they likely to notice a laser flash, nor— Never mind. You've got to have these men."

"For their own sakes, if nothin' else," Valland agreed. He leaned his ax against the table and folded his arms. "I can't believe you'd murder your fellow human bein's, Yo."

"Not willingly. Only if I absolutely must, and then in love and service. But they are hostages. They'll leave with us."

"Now you know I can't allow that. We'd never get 'em

back." Valland sought the gaze of the prisoners. "Hate to sound theatrical, but stayin' laconic is hard work. Which'd you rather be, dead or slaves?"

Sweat glistened on their skins. Galmer jerked out, "You needn't ask," and Bren nodded.

"You see," Valland told Rorn, "you can buy your own escape with their lives and freedom, but that's all."

Rorn looked uncertain. A splashing resounded from the tank, and the two great sleek heads broke surface. Through the scant illumination, chalcedony eyes probed at Valland. He gave them stare for stare.

The Ai Chun spoke via their dwarf. In the Earth-days since he renounced his species, Rorn had improved his command of Yonder until he could readily use it; so much does the removal of inward conflict do for the mind, and you may decide for yourself whether it's worth the price. "Do you follow them, Hugh?" he asked. "Not so well, eh? They say—" He stopped. "Do you know just what they are?"

"The skipper told me about them," Valland said shortly.

"He's prejudiced. They are . . . good, wise— No, those words are too nearly meaningless. . . . They are as far beyond us as we are beyond the apes."

"I'm not sure how far that is." Valland shrugged. "Go on, what do they want?"

"You've . . . we've caused them a heavy loss. This latest episode goes further to prove that they can't tolerate us running loose, any more than we could tolerate pathogenic bacteria. But they don't strike out, blindly destructive, as men would. They'll take us in. They offer us more than we could ever hope to gain, or know, or feel, by ourselves."

"Like your case?" Valland said. "Sorry, but I am bein' sarcastic. The answer is no. You and they can go in return for our friends. Then, if you all leave us be, we'll do the same for you."

Rorn translated. The Ai Chun were slow to reply, as they were slow to most things. In the end:

"Negative," Rorn said. "They don't fear death. They're reborn, immortal in a way we'll never achieve."

"Have you swallowed that crock yourself?"

"Makes no difference. I'm not afraid either, not of anything any longer. But think. It doesn't matter whether their belief is correct or not. What does matter is that they hold it. By taking these men away from you, whether by death or captivity, they'll ruin you. For the sake of that, they don't much mind cutting short a pair of incarnations."

"They'd better not mind." Valland grinned bleakly, "with their chums listenin' in."

"Don't you understand what that means?" Rorn breathed. "You aren't just confronting two individuals. An entire world! You can't win on your own terms. But let go your pride. It's no more than a monkey screaming from the treetops how important he is. Let go, use your reason, take their guidance, and you'll have our true victory."

"Spare me the sermon, Yo. I got a girl waitin' on Earth. The rest of us have our loves too, whatever they may be, as strong as yours. We'd sooner die than give them up. I've lived a fair spell, and it's been my observation that hate doesn't make for conflicts which can never be settled. People who hate each other can still strike bargains. But conflictin' loves are somethin' else."

Valland stood a while, stroking his beard and sunk in thought. Outside, the battle had ended. In the silence that now filled the hut, one grew aware of breathing, the faint lap of waves in the tank as the Ai Chun stirred, the thump of a spear butt on the floor, the heat and stenches and inward-crowding shadows.

Finally Valland gusted a sigh. He raised his head and spoke, low but resonant. "How about me?"

"What?" Rorn gaped at him.

"I organized this attack, you know. Modest as I am, I doubt if my gang is any military threat without me. If you must keep a hostage, suppose you take me instead of those fellows."

"No, Hugh!" Galmer cried.

"We can't afford heroics," Valland said to him. "You can spare my technical knowledge, at least. And maybe I can talk these people into makin' peace. Think you could?"

Bren thrust his face up, so that light could touch the lines and hollows lately carved therein. "*You* don't know what they're like," he said.

Valland ignored him. "Well?" he asked Rorn.

"I . . . I don't know." A conference followed. "They must consider this."

"All right," Valland said. "I'll leave you alone to talk the proposition over."

He started for the door. "Halt!" Rorn yelled. A soldier sprang in pursuit.

Valland obeyed, turned about and said evenly, "I've got to tell them outside in any event, and prove this is my personal idea. Otherwise you could get attacked soon's you cross the threshold. I'll come back in two, three hours and see what you've decided. Agreed?"

They stood dumb and let him depart.

XIV

VICTORY was dead meat in ya-Kela's mouth. Word had run through the Packs: There are actual downdevils here, now when God is withdrawn from heaven. Ya-Valland himself could not prevail against them, he left the house they have taken without those he went in to save, and however strange his kind may be to us, we can see, we can even smell the horror that clutches him and his mates. Day glares upon us. Best we slink off under the forest roof.

Many had already done so. And more and more of them followed, picking up their gear and vanishing into the mists. They spoke little, but that little made a mumbling across the land like the first wind-sough before a storm.

He himself was fain to leave. But because ya-Valland asked it, he used his last shreds of authority to hold some in place. A hundred or less, they squatted well away from the compound in a ring about such prisoners as had been taken. They dared not tend the dead of either side. Corpses littered the tussocky ground, rocked among the reeds, sprawled beneath the walls; and the carrion wings wheeled impatiently overhead.

Ya-Valland, ya-Argens, and ya-Urduga stood disputing in their own tongue, which no longer seemed likely to be God's. Ya-Kela waited, slumped down on heels and tail, feeling his age and his weariness. He had been given to understand that ya-Valland would go away with the downdevils as the price of liberty for his other two mates. But without him, what were the rest? They seemed to feel likewise, for the talk waxed fierce until ya-Valland cut it off and would listen to no more.

Then he addressed the One. He had fetched his music-maker. The Azkashi sounds limped forth: "Be not disheartened, my friend. We did not succeed as well as we hoped, but the hunt is far from ended."

"We have run ourselves breathless," ya-Kela said, "and the quarry swings about to gore us. Who may prevail against the downdevils save God, Who has forsaken the world?"

"I do not plan to stay with the enemy for long," ya-Valland said.

"They have taken captives often and often. None ever returned. Old stories tell of a few whom the Packs recaptured in skirmishes. They were so changed that naught could be done but kill them as gently as might be."

"I shall not suffer such a fate if you will stand by me."

"I owed you a blood debt," ya-Kela said, "but it has been paid with folk who were dear to me."

"You have not yet paid your debt to your people," ya-Valland said sharply.

Ya-Kela started, glanced up at him, and rose to bring their eyes more nearly level. "What do you mean by this newest riddle?"

"Something that you—all the Azkashi—must come to understand. Without it, you are doomed. With it, you have hope; more than hope, for when free folk know what freedom costs and how to meet that cost, they are hard indeed to overcome."

A faint tingle ran along ya-Kela's skin. "Have you a new magic for us?"

"Better than a magic. An idea." Ya-Valland sought words. "Listen to a story.

"In the sky-place whence I come were two countries. One was called Europe, where dwelt a people like myself. The other was called America, and a different folk possessed it whom we named Indians. The people of Europe crossed the waters between and started to take land in America. Most of the Indians were hunters. At best, they could not match the powers of the Europeans, who were not only farm-keepers like the Niao but also had new weapons. Thus, in time, the Europeans took all America away from the Indians."

Ya-Kela stepped back. His ax lifted. "Are you telling me that you are akin to the Herd?" he shouted.

Ya-Velland's mates clapped hands to those fiery weapons they had repossessed. He waved them back, spread his own empty hands, and said:

"In some ways, yes. In other ways, no. For example, the Indians held a faith in beings not unlike the downdevils, whereas the Europeans worshiped one God. I am trying to teach you a lesson. Are you brave enough to hear me out?"

Ya-Kela could say nothing but, "Yes." Lowering his ax was harder work than his charge into arrows and flame.

"For, you see," ya-Valland said, "the Indians need not have lost. In the early days, at least, they outnumbered the European settlers. They were masters of the wilderness. They were not slow to get for themselves weapons like those of the invaders. In truth, at times they had better ones, and inflicted numerous bloody defeats on their foe.

"Why, then, did they lose?"

"The reasons were several. But a great one was this. They were satisfied to win a battle. To them, any piece of land was as good as any other, provided both had game. They fought for honor and glory alone. If once a territory had been occupied, and farms had covered it, they did no more than raid its outskirts. And seldom did they stand and die like Europeans, to hold a place that was holy because their fathers were buried there.

"Furthermore, ya-Kela, they did not fight as one. If a Pack of them was overwhelmed, that was of small concern to other Packs elsewhere. Some even helped the Europeans against their own kinfolk. None thought of bringing the whole American land together, under a single council. None planned generations ahead, sacrificing lives and goods that their great-grandchildren might be free. All these things the Europeans did. And thus the Europeans conquered.

"Can you see what may be learned from this?"

Ya-Kela bowed his head. "The lesson is hard."

"I do not expect the Azkashi to learn it soon," ya-Valland said. "If you yourself do so in your lifetime, and teach a few others, that may suffice." He was still for a moment. "And perhaps then I will have paid a part of the blood debt my ancestors left me."

Ya-Kela cried in anguish, "What has this to do with your going away?"

"Only that, whatever becomes of me, you must think ahead and hold fast to common purpose. You must not be content with a single victory like ours today, nor lose your will because of a later defeat such as we have also met. I am the one who hazards the gelding of his souls, and I have not yet despaired. Be you likewise. God has not left you."

"Look in the sky and tell me so again," ya-Kela said.

"Why, I shall. Come here."

Ya-Valland led him into the compound, though he cringed from the silent, locked house. A lean-to behind held the enigmatic tools he had observed on his earlier visit. "We are lucky that we did not wish to be crowded by those in our living quarters," ya-Valland said. He took one, a box and tube mounted on three legs, and carried it back to free ground.

"This," he said, "we call a *photoscreen 'scope*. Suppose you have a very hot fire. Cast a small ember into the coals, and you will not be able to see it, for the coals flood it with their brilliance. Yet if the place were otherwise dark, the ember would seem bright enough. True?"

"True," ya-Kela said. Wonder began to take hold of him. The mere sight of magics like this gave spirit.

"The 'scope has the power to pluck faint lights out of greater," ya-Valland said. He consulted with his mates and a set of leaves covered with curious markings, and pointed the tube heavenward. "I will show you the sky—yonder part— as if night had fallen. See."

He touched a projection. A smooth flat plate on the box grew dark. One point of light burned near the middle.

"Is that not where the planet Oroksh should be?" ya-Valland asked. Ya-Kela assented mutely. As the One, he had long been intimate with the heavens. "Well, find me another." Ya-Kela gestured at unseen Ilyakan—if it really was there, his thought shuddered. Ya-Valland aimed in the same direction. "Hm, not quite right. Here." As he moved the tube, another steady spark drifted across the plate. "Do you see?"

"I see," ya-Kela said humbly.

"Now let us try low in the east."

Ya-Kela gasped, sprang back, fell to all fours and howled the first lines of the Welcome. God shone upon him. Ya-Valland twisted a knob, and God blazed brighter than mortal eyes had ever before seen Him.

"He is still aloft," ya-Valland said. "This you could well have known for yourselves, save that you would not agree that the sun could hide Him. Think, though. It does not mean He is less than the sun. A bonfire a great distance off may be veiled by a torch close to hand. Fear not the downdevils; God is with you yet."

Ya-Kela crouched on the wet earth and sobbed.

Ya-Valland raised him up and said, "I ask only courage of you, which you have already shown. We have little time before I must go back into the house. Let us make plans. Later you shall bring those hes whom you think will take this sight as you did. Then we shall be ready for whatever may befall."

He looked at his comrades. His teeth showed, in that gesture which seemed to betoken mirth among his breed, and he said in their language: *First time this gadget was used for religious purposes, I'll bet. Wonder if the manufacturer will be interested in buyin' an endorsement?"*

"Hugh," said ya-Argens, *"I don't know whether to call you a hero or a devil."*

Ya-Valland lifted his shoulders and let them fall. *"Neither,"* he said. *"Just a fanatic, for reasons you know."*

XV

THE BEST BARGAIN we could make was harder than awaited. We must release every Niao prisoner. And I too must become a hostage.

In exchange we got Bren and Galmer back, and kept the guns we had recaptured. Rorn was obviously satisfied. ("He's the real negotiator," Valland remarked. "The Ai Chun can't know beans about war or politics. So they kid themselves that they made him for the purpose.") We were the leaders. Without us, the Azkashi alliance must soon fall apart, after which the last three men could be picked off at leisure. Naturally, Rorn maintained the fiction that once in Prasiyo we would negotiate; and naturally we pretended to be taken in by it, less from logic than from wishful thinking.

Disarmed, burdened with our survival gear and a fresh food supply, we walked from the hut in the middle of a soldier cordon who held knives to our ribs. The weather had cleared for a while, though fresh thunderheads were piling up in the north, blue-black masses where lightning winked. The Ai Chun went before us. On land they were gross, clumsy, and still somehow terrible. A forlorn party stood to watch us off: Urduga, Bren, Galmer, an Azkashi handful. They scarcely stirred. Our compound seemed very small in that vast dark landscape.

Several canoes had been drawn ashore, along with the Pack dugouts. Rorn gave them a hard look. "Are these all you have?" he demanded.

"Yes," I said. "No doubt a number are drifting free, and probably others went home in panic."

"We'll be pretty crowded." Rorn spoke with his masters. Voiceless messages flew across the water. "A detachmant from Prasiyo will meet us, and we can transfer some of our party. But that can't be for many hours."

"Or we might come on one or two abandoned boats," Valland suggested. "I hope so. Don't fancy sittin' cheek by jowl, myself, when the jowls are so hairy." He took a long breath. "Ah-h-h! Even this Turkish bath air is good, after all that time in the cabin arguin' with you."

"You needn't have dragged matters out as you did," Rorn told him.

"Can't blame a fellow for tryin', can you?"

The canoes were long, with more than a meter of freeboard and great stability even after we filled them from stem to stern. To be sure, overloading much reduced their speed. The Ai Chun, who took ample room for themselves, could easily have run away from their escort. But we stayed together. Coxswains chanted low beneath the breeze, waves, distant muttering thunder; paddles bit; we started forth across the lake. My last clear glimpse of land showed me the men we had liberated, wading out among the reeds to stare and stare after us.

We three humans were in the same canoe. I hadn't expected that. But Rorn wanted to talk. We squatted as best we could near the bow, so that the other passengers only squeezed us from one side. They were mute, hardly moving save to nurse a wound or change a shift at the paddles. Their gods had come through for them, but they were still exhausted and shaken by what had gone before. As we passed the wreck of the *Meteor*, many signed themselves.

"Why didn't you bring your omnisonor, Hugh?" Rorn asked.

"I'm not exactly in a mood to sing," Valland grunted.

"But it'd be useful for communication."

"We got Yonder."

"Nevertheless—"

"Damnation!" Valland exploded. "That instrument made my song to Mary O'Meara. You think I'll use it for talkin' with your filthy owners?"

"Spare the emotion," Rorn said. "The Ai Chun have as much right to preserve their culture as anyone else does. You've done them harm enough."

Well, I thought, *I guess I am sorry that old Gianyi got killed. He was a decent sort, in his fashion.*

"We didn't set out to hurt anybody," Valland said. "If they'd left us alone, none of this would've happened."

"Oh? What about your effect on the savages? You planned to organize them, give them new techniques, whole new concepts. And they are the enemy. They'd have become a good deal more dangerous to the Niao. Furthermore, whatever your personal intentions, could you guarantee to keep men off this world indefinitely?"

"No," Valland said, "and I wouldn't care to anyhow. Your right of cultural self-preservation is a lot of belly rumble. Anybody's got a right to defend himself against attack, sure—which is what we were doin'. But his right to wall off new ideas comes from nothin' but his ability to do so. If he can make the policy stick, fine. That proves he's got something which works better than the so-called progressive notions. But if he can't, tough luck for him."

"In other words," Rorn jabbed, "might makes right."

"I didn't say that. Of course there are good or bad ways to compete. And if somebody doesn't want to play the game, he should be free to pot out. Only then he can't expect to be subsidized by those who do want to keep on playin'." Valland began to remove his boots and tunic. "Judas, it's hot! I could use some of that thundershower over there."

"The Ai Chun were ancient when we hadn't yet become

mammals," Rorn said. "Do you dare call yourself wiser than them?"

"Garden of Eden theory of history," Valland murmured.

"What?"

"Used to hear it often on Earth, a long time ago when things were still fermentin' there. People would look around at everything that was goin' wrong and blame it on the fact that men had left the good old tried-and-true ways of their grandfathers. I always thought, though—if those ways had been so fine, why were they discarded in the first place?"

"You mean," I ventured, "if the downdevils really are superior, they should have nothing to fear from us?"

"Right," Valland said. "Besides, speakin' of self-determination and so forth, how much has the Herd got?"

A trace of irritation crossed Rorn's features. Remembering how he had once snapped at us all, I felt a hideous kind of pity. This was like seeing a ghost.

"You may rationalize as much as you will," he said. "The fact is, the Ai Chun are proving their superiority at this moment."

"They've grabbed a temporary tactical advantage," Valland said. "We'll see how things work out in the long run. Just what do you propose to do?"

"Prevent the establishment of a base on this planet," Rorn said candidly. "Not by force, I think. There are better ways. We'll convince any future visitors that the planet is useless to them. I have some ideas along those lines."

"They'll need you, for certain, the downdevils," I agreed. "But how do they intend to keep you alive? You took along a supply of portable rations. But what about when those give out?"

"The food tanks are intact, back in camp," Rorn said. "Your friends won't refuse to feed you, even if it means feeding me too."

Until such time as you kill them and seize the units for yourself, I thought sickly.

"Why don't you peel down also, before you melt, skipper?" Valland asked.

The reminder was a shock. Heat weighed me down like thick wet wool. A strengthening breeze from the north gave small relief. In fact, if it blew us off our straight-line course, or those rising clouds covered the sun by which we were presumably navigating— I fumbled at my garments. My muscles felt stiff. *Won't do to be cramped,* I thought amidst a beating in chest and temples. *No room here for a real stretch, but a few isometrics ought to help.*

"Makes me remember the High Sierra," Valland mused.

"The what?" I asked. Anything was welcome that would make me forget for a while that I was here, and would quite likely soon be dead. But I don't know if he was really talking to me. He looked across the waters, into the murk of day and the livid storm, and almost he sang.

"Mountain section on Earth. Parts were kept as wilderness. Mary and I backpacked in there once. That was just before the antithanatic came along. But of course everybody knew it'd soon be in production. Nobody who was alive would have to grow old. Those were strange weeks. Thinkin' back, I have trouble makin' them seem real. The world had grown so quiet. Wasn't so much that people got extra cautious, knowin' what they stood to lose. It was an air. For a bit, while the human race waited, it felt kind of like wakin' after a fever had broken. All mankind, since first it began to think, had gone around with that sickness, the fear of old age. You'd look at a little girl, like yours, say, and you'd think of your grandmother, and know that in less'n a century this packet of happiness would be blind and in pain and hungry for death. Then suddenly we didn't have to take that any more. People needed a while to get used to the idea.

"Mary and I, though, we were young. We couldn't sit

still. We had to do somethin' to . . . to show ourselves we were alive enough to rate immortality. What'd be the use of it, if we only spent our centuries bein' careful? Eventually most people felt likewise, of course, and went to the stars. But we did from the first. Or, rather, Mary did—that kind of girl—and made me see it too.

"So we flitted to the Seirra, and loaded up, and started hikin'. Day after day; sun overhead, wind through the pines, till we got above timberline and looked down those tremendous blue slopes, crossed a pass and stopped for a snowball fight; and one night we camped by a lake where the moon and Jupiter rose together and threw two perfect glades, and Mary's the only sight I've seen that was more beautiful.

"Though, you know, we weren't simply havin' fun. To her, anyhow, and to me on her account, it was a sort of pilgrimage. Others had loved this place. But death got them and they'd never come back here. We wanted to do this for them. We swore to each other we'd always remember our dead." A small sad smile crossed Valland's lips. "Oh, Lord, but we were young!"

Rorn half opened his mouth. I bristled. How much more preaching could a man be expected to take? Precisely in time, a voice hailed from the leading canoe.

"Ya-o-o-o-a aie! Aie!"

The Niao shifted their packed bodies down the length of our boat and peered across the heads of their fellows. The soldiers among them laid hands on weapons. The paddlers stopped work. I heard the wind, still stiffening, pipe in my ears; little whitecaps slapped our hull and rocked it. Sliding my goggles off my brow and activating them, I also stared.

The gloom was made lighter for me and I saw another Herd canoe a few kilometers to the west. It wallowed alone without visible sign of life. But the dwarf shrilled on the vessel of the Ai Chun and his word was bayed thence by the giants.

"What're they sayin'?" Valland asked.

"People of ours in that craft," Rorn said. "Frightened . . . in pain, I believe . . . I haven't many words of Niao yet. The Ai Chun sense their minds."

And could not actually read the thoughts, leaped through my own brain. However, by now they must have studied humans enough that they can identify our basic emotional patterns too. If they should tune in on me, what would they observe?

I struggled to suppress the fear-hope-fury that churned in me. I might as well have told the approaching storm to go home.

"Survivors of the battle, evidently," Valland said. "Must've been wounded, escaped, haven't the strength to maintain headway." At a shouted command, our group veered and started moving anew. "Well, an extra boat should relieve the jam somewhat for us."

Could the Ai Chun tell Herd from Pack purely by mentalistics? I believed not. There was no real species difference. Ai Chun telepathy must be short-range and imprecise; otherwise they wouldn't have had to operate through the dwarfs. When you develop a tool, you don't evolve the tool's capability in yourself. Nor does it have yours. The dwarfs were specialized; they didn't keep watch or give warning unless told to. For millions upon changing millions of years, no one on this world had needed any equivalent of radar—nor, in the downdevils' omnipotence, the cruel tricks of war.

Such reasoning had been the basis of Valland's strategy, which had worked until he'd encountered Rorn. We must hope it remained sound.

Certainly the Ai Chun would notice rage and terror aboard that canoe. They should dismiss it as a natural aftermath of battle. Valland's and my flare of emotion, though— why should *we* get excited?

"Shut your hatch, you dog!" I yelled at Rorn.

"What in the universe?" He blinked at me.

"Talking about 'our people.' They aren't ours. Nor yours. You sold yours out!"

I made an awkward lunge at him. He fended me off. A soldier behind him prodded me back with his spear. Valland took my arm. "Easy, skipper," he said. To Rorn: "Not that I don't agree!" He added some obscenities.

"Be quiet," Rorn said. He smoothed his lank, wind-tossed hair. "I'll talk to you after you're fit to think."

A question was flung at him from his masters. He replied in Yonder. I could follow the exchange, more or less. "Nothing serious. The hostages got unreasonable."

Valland and I swapped a glance. We must not let ourselves feel relief. That might also be noticed.

"How do you expect us to do anything but hate your guts?" he growled.

"I said be quiet," Rorn answered. "I'll have you punished if you aren't."

We nurtured revengefulness like a cherished flower. The canoes crawled forward. Presently a Niao stood up in the distant one—how distant!—and waved. He was unmistakable, a soldier type, and hideously hurt. I didn't like to think of the means by which his cooperation had been gotten. *Not my idea or Hugh's,* I told myself, wishing that could justify me. *A flourish of ya-Kela's, I suppose. What do you expect, after the way his people have suffered?*

If time had seemed unbearably long before, it now became infinite. The gap between vessels narrowed as if we were on a hyperbola seeking its asymptote. I must have been half crazy when Valland's roar pierced the clamor in me:

"Look out!"

An order bawled through the wind at the same instant. Paddles stopped. Someone had observed something suspicious.

"Let's go!"

I sprang to my feet. We were not so close that I could look into the drifting boat. I knew that the several bodies huddled in the hull should not look different from ordinary Niao. But perhaps— The wounded soldier had collapsed.

Rorn snatched at me. My injured arm batted his hands aside, my good fist struck his face. The impact rammed back into my bones. A spear thrust at Valland. He sidestepped and dived overboard. I followed.

The water was warm and murky-red. I held my breath and pumped arms and legs until it was no longer possible. When my head must go up into air, Rorn's craft was still nearly on top of me.

Arrows smote the waves. I went below again and swam blind.

Now the Azkashi in the canoe revealed themselves, seized paddles and drove frantically to meet us. This had been Valland's idea: precarious indeed, but any chance was worth taking to escape what had been done to Rorn.

While the enemy was kept in the hut, bargaining, most of the captured Niao boats were taken off and hidden. A few were left, a number not so small as to be unlikely but small enough that they would be overburdened and slow. One went ahead, over the horizon, lightly manned with ya-Kela for captain.

Our men ashore took a compass bearing on the Ai Chun course. Hastily instructed, ya-Kela likewise had such an instrument, and a radio. Bren, Galmer, and Urduga could get a fix on him and tell him where to go lie in wait. And . . . his folk took along a couple of torchguns.

Their bolts flashed against a curtain of lightning as I re-emerged. Water puffed in steam; those were inexperienced hands on the triggers. Nonetheless, the Ai Chun group backed off.

Yet the enemy had not quit. Four huge forms sprang out

and started swimming. Adapted to a watery planet, those soldiers could overhaul us well before ya-Kela arrived. They could drag us back—at the least, kill us. My strength was already going. I am not much of a swimmer.

Valland was, by human standards. But when he saw the shapes churning after, he came about. His powerful crawl brought him to me in a couple of minutes. "Tread water," he panted. "Conserve your energy. You'll need it."

"We're done," I choked.

"Maybe. Maybe not. Better this way, anyhow."

The nearest soldier darted ahead. Valland got between me and him. They clinched and went under.

A hand closed on me. I looked into the open muzzle, tried weakly to break loose, and was submerged myself. It roared in my head. I thought confusedly, *Breathe water, you fool. Drown and die free.* But reflex was too strong, I gasped, spluttered, and whirled toward night.

My face was back in the air. I was being towed. Valland came alongside. He had broken his opponent's neck, down in the depths. He used his thumbnail, twice. The soldier ululated and let me go.

Valland must support me. The remaining pair closed in, through the stained waves. He used his legs to move away from them. They swam around to his head. I saw a dagger lifted.

Then the water was full of bodies and weapons.

Ya-Kela's were also good swimmers. Half a dozen of them had plunged the moment they'd seen our plight. Outpacing any canoe in their sprint, they got to us. Their comrades were not so far behind; and while the gunners dared not shoot near us, they could prevent any reinforcements from coming.

I did not see the fight. Darkness took me once more.

—Afterward I lay in the canoe, vomited, coughed, and wept. It wasn't merely reaction. I was altogether sickened. Galaxy God—any God—must we kill through all time, until time ends when the disgusted universe collapses inward on us?

Worse followed. I am glad I was only hazily aware. With yells of joy, the Azkashi gave chase to the Ai Chun. We were soon so close that a marksman like Valland could pick them off. One reached the water and went below, but he waited until the creature rose to breathe and shot him.

The storm rolled upon us. Clouds drove black across the sun, lightning blazed, thunder crashed, the first rain whipped my bare skin. I looked across the gunwale to Yo Rorn's boat, which we were now pursuing to reclaim our gear. My goggles still worked. I saw him stand up, screaming, such agony in him that it was almost good when a soldier's ax broke open his skull.

Valland hunkered beside me. Water ran over his cheeks, into his beard, like tears. "I never intended that," he said dully. "They must've gone insane, seein' me kill their gods. They had to strike back, and he was the handiest." He watched the boats scatter and flee. The one we were after was abandoned by those left in it. "Thanks for that. No more slaughter needed. . . . You were one of us too, always, Yo."

"But why did you kill the Ai Chun?" I blubbered. "We were safe by then. Why?"

"We're not safe," he answered. "Won't be for a mighty long time. I reckoned it'd make a good lesson for everybody concerned, to see they can be struck down like anyone else. We'll need everything we can get workin' for us."

He shook himself. "No use in regrets," he said. "We've got to be ruthless, or surrender right now. I suppose there are limits to what we can decently do, but I don't think we've reached 'em yet. Come, skipper, you'll feel more cheery after a good long sleep. Let's get on home."

XVI

Day stood at afternoon. We had rested, repaired damage, started to organize ourselves afresh, and slept some more. Nonetheless, when we stepped out of our compound and saw the lake glow red in that purple twilight, we had a sunset feeling. A great hush lay on the land. Further down the shore twinkled the fires of ya-Kela's people. Most Pack members had gone home after a skyhooting victory celebration for which many returned from the woods; but he stayed with some. We were to join them and lay plans.

For a while, just beyond the gate, we paused. Valland, Bren, Galmer, Urduga, and me—we seemed terribly few.

Galmer voiced what we thought. "Do you really believe we have a chance?"

"Why sure," Valland said. His gaiety was strange to hear in so big and dark a place. "We've got our camp back. Nothin' was ruined that we can't get along without. We have allies. Son, if we don't get home again, we won't deserve to!"

"But the enemy, Hugh. The Ai Chun. They won't take this like sportsmen. They'll come against us. We can't stand off a planet."

"We'll have our problems, all right," Valland admitted. "But think. We've shown the Packs you can beat the down-devils. So they'll go with us through a supernova, if only we handle them right, and I reckon I know how." His gaze went across the broad waters. "Distance makes a good defense. Any attackers' line of communications will get stretched thin. Woodsrangers like ours can cut it in two. Though I don't aim

117

to sit and wait. I'm takin' the offensive soon's may be. We'll burn Prasiyo, lay the countryside waste everywhere around, chase the Herd clear to the sea. The downdevils aren't used to actin' fast, I gather. So they'll need some time to recover from that shock and mount a counterattack. By then we'll be ready."

"Still," I said, "a war— When can we do our work?"

"Not our war," Valland said. "Mainly the Packs are concerned. We'll give them leadership, new kinds of weapons, sound tactics, a concept of strategy. I think that'll suffice. Remember, there can't be an awful lot of Herd soldiers. The downdevils never needed many, and won't have time to breed a horde—which they couldn't supply anyhow. No, for the most part we should be free to work, we and the ones we're goin' to train as helpers."

After a moment, reflectively, he added: "Won't be a war of extermination anyhow. Our side'll be content to hold this territory, maybe get back some of what was stolen before; but the Packs aren't about to try conquerin' the world. If the downdevils aren't hopelessly stupid, they'll make terms, once we've rubbed their noses a bit. Then we five can really buckle down to business."

Bren sighed. The weight of his captivity was still heavy on him. "That's assuming we're not killed in some fracas," he said. "More, it's assuming we can stay with our purpose. I wonder if we won't get so tired at last that we'll simply quit."

Valland squared his shoulders. The light turned his shock head to copper. Huge against the sky, he said, "No, we won't. We'll keep ourselves reminded of what this is all about—what we're goin' back to."

He started toward the campfires, and striding, he keyed the omnisonor he bore to help him talk with the Pack, and his song arose.

"So softly you hear it now, Mary O'Meara, but soon it

comes joyful and clear.
And soon in the shadow and dew of your hilltop a
star-guided footfall rings near.
My only beloved, I'm here."

We followed him. And we built our spaceboat and won to the help of the Yonderfolk. The job took four decades.

XVII

(Thus far the account published by Guild Captain Felip Argens in his autobiography. An additional tape was found among his effects by the redactor of the posthumous edition.)

EARTH IS A QUIET WORLD.

Oh, yes, wind soughs in the great forests that have come back, now that so few people live there; birds sing, cataracts brawl, the oceans rush on the moon's trail around the globe. You can find ample enjoyment in the starport towns, and the educational centers are bright with youth from every part of the galaxy. Nor is this a museum planet by any means. The arts flourish. Science and scholarship are live enterprises.

But there is too much of the past. One does not build new things there, one preserves the old. That isn't bad. We need traditions. From a strictly practical standpoint, it's good to know you can leave your Earthside property in charge of some robots, return in five hundred years, and find not only it but its surroundings unchanged. Nevertheless, when the adventurers come from the stars on a visit, they walk quietly.

Hugh Valland and I parted in Niyork. Bren, Galmer, and Urduga had gone their separate ways. I had to report, however, and he had his girl, so we traveled together on the *Luna Queen*. Though he'd avoided discussing his plans in detail, I assumed he'd be met when the ferry set us down.

"No," he said. "That's not her way. How about one hell of a good so-long dinner tonight? I know a restaurant where the escargots consider themselves privileged to be cooked."

He was right. We put away a lot of wine too. Over brandy and cigars, in a fine comradely warmth, I asked if he meant to take as lengthy a vacation as I did.

"Mmm—probably not," he said. "We were stuck on that single planet for such a confounded chunk of time. I've got a universeful of places to go see again. And then new places, where nobody's been yet."

"D'you mean to sign on for exploration?" I raised my eyebrows. "I hoped you'd ship with me."

His massive face crinkled in a smile. "Skipper," he said, "you're a fine chap, but don't you think we need to split up for a century or two?"

"Maybe." I was disappointed. True, we'd lived in each other's breath long enough to drive anyone who wasn't immortal, who couldn't set the years in perspective, to murder. But we'd fought and worked together, and laughed and sung and hoped: and he was the one who had kept us doing so. Having a war on our hands had been a help—broke the monotony, Valland used to say—but we wouldn't have won it without his leadership. I didn't want to lose touch.

"You'll be around for a while, anyway, won't you?" I asked.

"Sure," he said. "What'd you think was drivin' me?"

"Mary O'Meara," I nodded. "What a girl she must be. When do I get an introduction?"

"Well, now . . . ." For the first time I saw him evasive. "Uh, that won't . . . won't be so easy. I mean, I'd like to, but—well, she's not keen on guests. Sorry. How about another cognac?"

I didn't press him. We had learned, out beyond the galaxy, not to intrude on a man's final privacies. I speculated, of course. Every immortal develops at least one quirk. His was that fantastic monogamy which had saved us. What was hers?— Then Valland's grin broke loose again and he related a couple of jokes he'd heard, bumming around in the rim-planet town where we waited for passage to Earth. We said goodnight in a hilarious mood.

After that, for several days, I was busy at the universarium. The scientists wanted to know everything about the planet of our shipwreck. They'd be sending a mission there, to operate out of the commercial base our company would establish. Before the unique Ai Chun culture died—before that race adapted to reality and became just another race—they meant to study it.

When I finished, I must return to Niyork on business. The Guild had suddenly decided our employers owed us a bonus for our troubles. A rather disgruntled chief accountant told me the sum, which explained his disgruntlement, and put me through various formalities.

"Payments are required to be made directly to the men," he said. With so many people on so many planets, the Guild no longer trusts the mails. "I've arranged about the others, but when I called Master Valland, he wasn't at the address he had given. It was a hotel here in town, and he'd moved out with no forwarding code."

"Gone to see his girl, of course," I said. "Hm. We plan to get together once more, but not for some while."

"Can't you find him before then? Frankly, I'm tired of having your association ride me about this matter."

"And Hugh'd no doubt find good ways to spend the money. Won't be so useful to him on the eve of shipping out." I pondered. From time to time he had said things about Mary O'Meara, though now that I added them together they came to surprisingly little. "Well, I'm at loose ends for the moment. I'll see if I can track him down."

That was for my own sake as well as his. To the company I wasn't a hero, I was a captain who had lost his ship. I wanted to get back into favor, or they'd put me on some dreary shuttle run for the next fifty years.

I walked into the street. Little traffic moved—an occasional groundcar, a few pedestrians. The tall towers that walled me in were mostly empty, ivy and lichen growing on their facades. Though the sun was glorious, the sun of Manhome, light seemed only to drown in that stillness.

Let's marshal the facts, I told myself. *She lives on, what's the name, yes, the coast of Maine. A historic but microscopic residential community. He never did say which one, but can't be many these days that fit. I'll check with data service, then run up and inquire. Do me good to get out in the country-side anyway.*

As things developed, the search robot gave me just one possibility. I rented a flitter and headed north. The woods have swallowed this part of the continent, I flew above green kilometer after kilometer. Dusk fell before I reached my goal.

That village was built when men first fared across the ocean which rolled at its feet. For a while it was a town, alive with lumberjacks and whalers. Then men moved west, and afterward they moved to the stars, and now a bare two hundred dwelt here: those curious, clannish folk who—even more than on places like Landomar—are not interested in worlds out yonder, who use their immortality to sink deeper roots into Earth.

I parked on an otherwise deserted carfield and walked downhill into town. Behind me lifted a birch forest; white trunks gleamed in twilight, and the air was fragrant with their leaves. Before me lay the few houses, peak-roofed, shingle-walled, their windows shining yellow. And beyond them reached the sea, and the first stars of evening.

A passerby directed me to the civil monitor's house. His name, Tom Saltonstall, suggested how old he must be. I found him seated on the porch in a rocking chair, smoking a pipe, while his one wife prepared dinner. He greeted me with polite reserve. There was something about him— After a minute I recognized it. He looked as youthful as I did; but he had the manner of beings I have met who cannot be immortalized and have grown gray.

"You want Hugh Valland?" he said. "Yes, sure, we know him." He squinted at me through the dimness before adding, with each word chosen beforehand: "A very decent fellow."

"I ought to realize that!" I exclaimed. "I was his captain this last trip. Hasn't he told you what happened?"

"Yes. A little." Saltonstall looked relieved. "Then you understand about— Sure. I'm sorry I didn't identify your name, Captain Argens. I'm overdue for mnemonic treatment. He's spoken fine of you, sir. An honor to meet you." He made the archaic handclasp with me. "Would you pleasure us by staying to eat?"

"Well, thanks, but I ought to find Hugh. Where is he?"

"He owns a house, next street down, third from the left corner. You won't find him there, though. He'll not be back till late, on a night like this."

Ah-ha! I grinned to myself; for the full moon was casting her foreglow into the eastern sky.

I wish I had stayed, and talked with the monitor and his wife. But I only expected the gossip of the Earthbound, which was tedious to me. Pleading weariness, I returned to my flitter. It had bunk, bath, and food facilities. I'd call on Valland tomorrow.

But after dinner I got restless. The multisense programs that I tuned in were not for a spaceman. The moon was up, throwing a broken bridge across the waters and turning the birches to silver. Crickets chirred, almost the only sound beneath those few stars that weren't hidden by moon-haze. This was Manhome. No matter how far we range, the salt and the rhythm of her tides will always be in our blood. I decided to go for a walk.

A graveled road wound further uphill, and scrunched softly under my feet. As I neared the forest, the live green smell strengthened. Dew glittered on long grass. Beyond the village, now dark, the sea murmured.

And then another tone lifted. For a moment, blindingly, I was back in a sinister red-lit crepuscule where nothing but those chords and that voice gave me the will to fight on. "Hugh!" I cried, and broke into a run.

He didn't hear me. I rounded a copse and saw where I was bound, just as he finished. The last stanza he had never sung to us.

> *"Sleep well once again if you woke in your darkness, sleep knowin' you are my delight*
> *As long as the stars wheel the years down the heavens, as long as the lilies bloom white.*
> *My darlin', I kiss you goodnight."*

I huddled into the thicket and cursed myself. He walked past me, down to his house, as proudly as on that day when our new-built boat first went skyward.

After a while I continued my walk. Ahead of me stood a small building with a steeple, white under the moon. White, too, were the flowerbeds and the stones among them. I searched till I found the one I was after. It must often have been renewed, in the course of eroding centuries. But the inscription was unchanged, even to letter style and dating. Not that there was much. Only

MARY O'MEARA
2018 - 2037

I believe I managed to confront him the next day as if nothing had happened.

Here's a quick checklist of recent releases of

ACE SCIENCE-FICTION BOOKS

F-titles 40¢   M-titles 45¢   G-titles 50¢

If you are missing any of these, they can be obtained
directly from the publisher by sending the indicated sum,
plus 5¢ handling fee, to Ace Books, Inc. (Dept. MM),
1120 Avenue of the Americas, New York, N.Y. 10036

CLASSICS OF GREAT SCIENCE-FICTION
from ACE BOOKS